ICE COOPER
AND THE
BEAST OF BALE

J A BOWLER

First Published by Springtail 2022

ISBN 978-1-8380512-3-5

Cover design by J A Bowler

Dedicated to all those who try to save us from the fire.

Chapter 1 ~ Horse

Daniel was fiddling with his pencil, tapping it on the desk repeatedly until it made Ice want to scream. She would never do that though, even if shouting, "Please Stop!" might have alleviated some of the dullness of the lesson. To the outside world, she lived up to the saying: *'Ice by name and Ice by nature'*. It was meant to be short for Isis, but the nickname suited her. Or at least the version of her that most people saw.

Instead, she rested her chin in her hands so that she could stick her fingers in her ears, and she stared resolutely out of the window to the field beyond the school gate. In the past she had appreciated the routine and the steady information flow of her classes in Year 10 at Depton High School, but it was getting harder to care. Not only was the class only half full, but many of those who were there, were struggling to concentrate – a combination of just not having had quite enough to eat recently and a new teacher who hadn't bothered to gauge the knowledge level of the pupils. There had been three different Physics teachers in this first half term and they all seemed to go over the same stuff without finding out what had already been taught. She thought of all the students who'd had this lecture through the three hundred years since Newton. First law, second law, third law... all the laws hadn't stopped people ignoring the warning signs, had they?

She gazed at the countryside. Some green remained, and too many people were still trying to convince themselves that everything would be fine. A year and a half ago, that spring had been the wettest on record. Torrential rain had fallen almost unceasingly and now, as if to wipe that memory, the heat of two consecutive summers was threatening to set the dry October countryside aflame. The trees just didn't quite know it yet. Their remaining leaves, now mostly yellow and red, were a testament to the water they could still tap with their deep roots, but the grass had long since gone the colour of straw and was trodden into dust on the school field.

She was surprised to see a multitude of birds weaving their patterns against the horizon. Last year's rain had given them a temporary banquet in an explosion of flies and mosquitoes. People had complained about the insects, but Ice did not share their view. Most species were not so lucky and she despaired at their absence and for those animals that depended on them. So it was a welcome sight and a thrill to behold this flock, the way they swooped and folded together, like a single organism, darkening as they clustered and fading at the edges as they spread out.

She stared, watching them draw closer together, until they seemed to form a solid mass and then, with a flash of astonishment that quickened her pulse, she saw it take on a definition – a shape that suddenly, uncannily, resembled a huge, black horse stamping its front hooves and rearing up against the afternoon sky.

"Daniel, look!" Ice whispered to her desk partner, nudging him and pointing urgently at the scenery beyond the window.

"Mm. Wow! Nice," he said, stopping the tapping of his pencil, to see what she was pointing at. "A murmuration?" He grinned at her. "Brilliant! Great when they do that isn't it?"

Ice frowned in frustration. Her friend hadn't seen the giant horse. By the time he had looked up, the birds had dispersed again and were making their normal patterns against the blue.

She sighed. Very little could be *strange* to Ice any more. She was becoming used to noticing things that other people just weren't aware of. After the shadelings – the dark creatures she had encountered last year – she was unlikely to be disturbed by much. They were ethereal little inhabitants between dimensions, that had taken her into the very fabric of the earth and shown her where to find a lost boy. Ice remembered her alarm at first when she had seen the small, black, cat-like forms climbing the clock tower the day she arrived in Depton.

They had plagued her childhood dreams but the real shadelings had turned out to be not what she had thought. It was human actions that had driven them to the surface and they were not a threat. Rather, they had helped Ice. She hoped they were OK now that the fracking had stopped.

It was odd how things could seem so normal. The family was back together and her mum was home. The stiffness in Ice's shoulder was only an occasional reminder of the injury she had sustained during the earthquake. The school and Joe seemed to have forgotten the incident where she had hit him with the metal tray. He had sort of deserved it for bullying little Nathan, but Ice had so far managed to stick to her resolution to never again resort to physical violence. That kind of melt-down was not a productive thing.

Daily lives went on and people chose to ignore the things they did not want to face. She closed her eyes and took a deep breath. Every time she had these thoughts, Ice had to quell the sick feeling of panic that rose from the pit of her stomach. Why were they sitting in this room listening to old, long-proven theories? Humanity was in peril. Not just humanity – the liveable earth was threatened. The evidence wasn't just a lot of scientific data – it was a daily slap in the face. Ice did not know what she expected the adults to do, but it was stunning how they could carry on as though it wasn't happening. People continued adjusting their ideas of 'normal', pretending it would all be fine, but it was a charade.

Chapter 2 ~ Witch

Joe was on the cycle path on the way back from school; Ice was not paying sufficient attention and had to squeeze her brakes hard to avoid knocking into him. Since the events that spring, they had formed a kind of uneasy truce but she was still bothered by him. She didn't understand why he was interested in hanging around and her first, bad impression of Joe was hard to shake. But then he had almost certainly saved Ice's life on the night of the earthquake, when they were both looking for Nathan at the stone circle. She owed him – she knew that.

"Alright?" he said to her, more as a casual greeting than a question. Ice nodded. Joe's face was pale and pinched, as usual, but at least the heat of the day meant he wasn't wearing his hoodie. Though his hair was dirty and unkempt, he looked a lot better with it not plastered to his face in dripping spikes as it had the day that Nathan had gone missing, when they had stood on the bridge in the pouring rain, looking into the furious river below.

She was trapped now. He was speaking to her and, to her own annoyance, she felt compelled to dismount and walk next to him as he made his way home.

"Seen any more of the… things?" he asked. Joe knew about the shadelings. He was one of the few. She had never told the adults about how she had known where to find Nathan and her boxer dog, Buddy. Ice wasn't sure what Joe had seen that night – whether the shadelings had been apparent to him – he hadn't said, but when she had visited him later, he had nodded along to her explanation as though it made sense to him.

"I haven't seen them," she replied and then hesitated before continuing, "But something else happened today that I can't explain. Why is Depton so weird?"

Joe gave a brief snigger.

"Are you sure it isn't *you* that is weird?" he asked before quickly continuing, "OK, OK, I know. Go on… what were you going to say?"

Ice paused. Did she want to go on? She wondered why she was even telling him anything. Sharing things with people was new to her. It was probably a good development, but she still did not find it easy. Somehow she could nearly always sense when people were lying – or at least trying to hide the truth. It was her 'superpower' and one that she often wished she didn't have. Conversations were frustrating – what was the point in opening up if people were going to be dishonest? And they so often were. So she mostly kept her thoughts to herself. It was why she preferred the company of animals. But recent events had shown her the importance of having friends who could actually talk back and offer support.

She briefly wondered if Joe counted as a 'friend'. He was certainly something more than an acquaintance but she didn't even really like him. She told him about what she had seen out of the science classroom window.

"An actual horse?" he queried with a short laugh. "Not just a horse-shape – you know, like people see things in the clouds? Dragons and praying angels and… you know...para… thingy."

"Para… pareidolia or something isn't it?" she replied. "When our brains make stuff we recognise out of random shapes. Faces on Mars and Jesus in the toast and whatever. This just looked so much more obvious than that. But maybe… anyway, when Daniel looked, it had turned back into a flock of birds, so...”

Joe nodded. “Ah yes. How is the blond bff?” he asked, laughing, but with just a detectable edge that Ice chose to ignore. He knew how Daniel was. Though Joe was in the year above Ice and her friends, he passed them nearly every day in the dining hall at school. It was a cheeky question just to get a reaction – which she didn’t give him.

They walked in silence until the junction of Joe’s road. Ice was slightly unsure as to the next move. In the past, she would have ridden off without a backward glance, not even realising that it was rude. These days she had a greater sense of what you were supposed to do, and that made her hesitate. Before she could figure out the right protocol, Joe cut in.

“Er… do you fancy not going home, yet?” he asked.

“What do you mean?” Ice replied, trying to fathom this new suggestion. She was on her way home. Why would she ‘fancy’ not going there? She understood the words, well enough, but not the subtext – the reason for the question.

“I dunno. I just... well it’s still really light...” he went on. “I don’t feel like going in yet.”

“I’ve got to get back to walk Buddy,” Ice said, flatly. “I can’t keep him waiting much longer.”

“Perfect! I’ll come with. I like dogs.”

Ice frowned at him. Joe had a brashness that she almost envied. *He* didn’t worry about the right thing to do, as if he was quite indifferent to the opinions of others. He was known for being the master of back-chat in school and frequently made responses the other children wouldn’t have dared. The teachers apparently did not intimidate him. Sometimes he caused them to seethe with fury or lose their tempers and shout. On other occasions, they laughed out loud. Right now, Joe had that familiar cocky air about him – the demeanour she remembered from their first meeting. She could do without it and moreover, she could sense the confidence was not authentic. Was that a hint of desperation behind his questioning grin? Without actually agreeing to his suggestion, she shrugged and let him tag along.

Buddy was bouncing by the time they got to the front door of Ice's house. Oscar hadn't arrived back yet and their dad was out, but Ice rightly assumed her mother was upstairs because she emerged from the 'office' and greeted the two children just visible from the landing.

"Sorry, Ice. I lost track of time. Are you going to be OK to walk Buddy? Oh, Hello..." The last part was directed at Joe. Her mum had only met him briefly after the accident and there was a note of curiosity in her voice which Ice found irritating.

"I'm just taking him now. This… er… Joe is…he wants to come for the walk." It sounded as awkward as Ice felt but her mum just nodded her thanks and told them both to take care.

Ice grabbed the boxer dog who was doing his normal thorough investigation of the newcomer, pushing his flat face into Joe's hand. She expected Buddy to become over-excited; he was usually a great test for a person's character. Nervous energy in a human, even when masked, always made Buddy a little bit naughtier. If he jumped up on someone, it was a good chance they were an anxious or excitable person. She was surprised to see that he was behaving quite well with Joe, who had dumped his bags by the coat-hooks and was crouched down at dog-level to stroke the fur on Buddy's head.

***

The route Ice took was one familiar to both children. When they reached the canal, safe from traffic, she unclipped the lead and let Buddy run ahead.

"He's a pretty cool dog," Joe said. "How are you managing to keep him fed?"

It was a good question. So far they had not run out of their stockpile of dog-food and were eking it out with whatever else they could find, but it was a worry. There was no knowing how much would be available in the shops and when. People were concerned about their own needs when there were food shortages. Animals were not a priority and already pets were being dumped, abandoned to their own fate. The local shelter did its best, but was struggling to feed them all. Ice knew that they had started to 'euthanise' unclaimed dogs, despite their previous claim that no healthy animal would ever be put down.

"We're managing," she replied. "My dad's friend has a smallholding – like a mini farm. He catches rabbits. There are still plenty of them by the river where the grass hasn't died – poor little guys. I don't want them to be killed, but... you know..."

"Yeah," Joe replied. "Not many vegans left, eh?"

Ice nodded. Some vegetables were available, of course, particularly if you had a friend who grew them – potatoes, leaks, sweetcorn. But it was never enough and the floods in the spring had done a lot of damage. Even though people had originally stored tins and dry food when they knew that there were going to be shortages, everyone was aware these were rapidly diminishing. If meat was available, people ate it. Hungry people are less fussy and only the rich weren't hungry.

They reached the entrance to the 'Twelve Brothers' standing stones – a neolithic circle in the middle of a grassy field. The earth was still scarred from the earthquake, and one of the stones had fallen, embedding itself in the mud of the storm.

In other ways, the scene had changed considerably. Where the wheat had been stubby and green, growing from a sodden, boggy terrain, it had now become brown and brittle, leaving behind a baked clay, covered in deep cracks, formed by the contraction of the soil as it dried. Ice allowed herself a brief, wry grin at Joe and he returned it with an up-tilted nod of the head. They both knew, without needing to speak, that this was common territory – the spot where he had pulled her to safety that night. She clambered on to the fallen stone as Joe joined her – a vantage point to watch Buddy who was enjoying snuffling through the remaining undergrowth that bordered the field.

"A bit different, isn't it?" she said to him. "I think I prefer it without the thunderstorm and the earthquake. Though I never thought we'd get to the point where we were wishing for some more rain."

"Yeah. What do they say? It never rains but it pours. Well it did pour. And now it never rains!" He leaned back on the palms of his hands and closed his eyes, lifting his head so that the heat of the afternoon sun fell directly on his face. Ice drew up her knees and hugged them, resting her chin on her arms and examining the boy who was next to her. She hadn't noticed earlier how thin he was. He had never been very bulky, but now she could see the outline of his ribs under his shirt, and the hollow dip of his torso below them as he stretched back. She noticed that the belt that was threaded through his trousers had been taken down a notch and the trouser fabric at the top was creased and buckled instead of stretched tight. As if becoming aware that she was staring at him, he turned his head and opened one eye at her, raising a brow as a wordless question.

"Are you OK?" she asked. "Do you still have enough stockpile?"

Joe's answer, whatever it might have been, was interrupted by Buddy's bark and they both looked up to find that they were no longer alone.

"Buddy, come!" Ice called, pretty certain that he would ignore her. She wasn't worried that he would harm anyone, but people were often stupid where dogs were concerned – particularly if they were large dogs with brindled patterns, it seemed.

"It's OK, he's safe!" she called to the woman who had entered the field. "He's just really friendly!"

This was the part of owning a dog that she disliked the most – having to deal with other members of the public. The woman walked towards them, lifting her hands in the air each time Buddy attempted to lick them. It was a mistake; to the dog, the game had just ramped up a notch and now involved jumping to try to grab the woman's cuffs. Ice swore under her breath and slid off the rock, going over to hold Buddy by the collar, clipping on the lead and giving him a tap on the neck to warn him to stop. It was only partly successful. The dog stopped jumping, but he was clearly excited by this stranger and Ice had to clamp his hindquarters between her knees to stop him pulling away.

"Sorry," she said. "He thinks you're playing."

The woman glanced down at Buddy and then peered at Ice. She looked like she was in her 40s, with thick, straw-coloured hair tending to grey. She had let it grow long and it was in need of a good conditioner and a bit of a brush. Ice noticed that in spite of the heat of the late afternoon, the woman had on a faded, green dress that reached to the ground. It was sleeveless, but she wore it over a mustard-coloured woollen jumper with frayed cuffs – the ones Buddy had found so tempting to grab. The woman shook her head at Ice and pointed at Joe and then back at her.

"You children should not be here. This is a sacred place and Samhain approaches. The fabric between the worlds grows thin. Things are awry on this Earth and the old spirits are restless." She seemed to shiver despite the sun, and clasped her upper arms as though she felt cold. "You!" she said staring more intently at Ice, "You have seen the Old Ones. Have you not heeded their warnings? Evil arises from our careless deeds and threatens us all. Nothing is as it was and all is in danger."

Ice backed off a little, pulling Buddy away. She glanced over at Joe, her expression a silent request that they should leave. She might be harmless enough, but her words to Ice made her stomach lurch. She had never met this person before – how did she know what Ice had seen? She told herself that the woman was probably a bit unhinged – maybe she was suffering the effects of hunger.

"No," she replied, shaking her head. She felt a flush of heat at her denial of the truth. "I don't know. We're going now." She began to walk quickly away, pulling Buddy on the lead, while Joe jogged to catch her up. Ice glanced back once when she reached the gate to the field. The strange woman was standing still in the middle of it and staring at the retreating children. Her scruffy hair and clothes gave her a wild look like a witch from an old film.

"What was that?" Joe laughed. "One of Depton's crazies?" He gave an exaggerated shudder. "Creepy! What did she say to you?"

"Nothing," Ice lied, increasing the pace of her walk along the canal. "It was nonsense." The woman had sounded crazy, but Ice's heart was pounding. She could not dismiss her impression that the woman had spoken truthfully.

Ice's father returned with a bag of potatoes from his farmer friend and Joe stayed for dinner. He wasn't invited, but he hung around, ignoring hints that they really had to get on and wouldn't his mother be expecting him, until the Coopers gave in and let him share the microwaved baked spuds with the remaining packet of cheese from their stores. From the way he attacked his food, it looked like it was the best meal he'd had in a while.

On his way out, Ice's mum pressed a small bag of potatoes into his hand.

"It's OK," she said. "We have plenty and you looked like you enjoyed your dinner! We can share fresh food with each other. Pay it back when you get a windfall yourselves."

Joe left hurriedly in the fading light. He seemed unable to summon a jokey response.

Once her mother had shut the front door, Ice ran upstairs quickly. She suspected that Oscar, who had looked bright-eyed and inquisitive all evening, was going to start an interrogation about their guest, and she didn't want to enter that territory. Nevertheless, she admitted to herself that she had been glad of Joe's company, particularly in the presence of the witch woman.

"Guys, fill the bottles, please. The water has just come back on!" This was their father's instruction as he tapped on Ice's door. The water company had begun limiting the supply to the evenings in an attempt to reduce the drain on the dwindling resources. So much rain had fallen last year, it was difficult to understand why their reserves were not full. But since then, they'd had two summers of uncommon heat and the water had disappeared quickly. Rivers which had been white, foaming torrents, were now low between the banks and in some places, just a trickle through a muddy bed exposing the tangle of rusting bicycles and shopping trolleys people had thrown in. The government which had made so many promises during the election, was showing itself to be not able or not willing to tackle the extremes of weather.

Money had been provided for the farmers, but that hadn't saved their crops. International trade was affected by political wrangling as well as droughts, floods and widespread forest fires and for the first time since the 1950s, food was rationed for most people. As always, when things were short, there was a thriving black market. People with lots of money or something desirable to trade, were able to continue to buy up what they wanted for themselves, or for resale at twice the price.

Oscar and Ice dutifully refilled their bottles. There was enough, too, for a quick shower but baths had been banned, along with the use of the hosepipe for anyone who was still trying to save their garden. Places like hospitals and schools were prioritised and had water when they needed it, but smallholders, like her father's friend, were only allowed to water their crops in the evening when the worst of the heat had abated.

Lost in thought, watching the water rise in the plastic container, Ice did not notice her mother looking at her until she glanced up briefly. Mrs Cooper was leaning in the doorway to the kitchen where Ice held the bottle under the flowing tap. She smiled as Ice caught her gaze.

"You OK?" she asked. "School and stuff?" Ice nodded and shrugged.

"Yes. I'm fine," she replied with a small huff of air that wasn't quite a laugh. "School's fine. A bit dull at times but they're doing their best, I suppose."

"I finally heard from the Crown Prosecution Service. I've got to give evidence next week."

Ice stared at her mother briefly and then sighed and shook her head.

"All that work you did to gather evidence against them! The earthquakes and the bad water. Surely there's no way they're going to get away with it, is there?"

Mrs Cooper shook her head slowly.

"I hope not. They've got the money for the fancy lawyers and the backroom deals, though. Who knows? Whatever happens, we stopped the fracking – I can't see them being able to start again any time soon – and it forced me to change jobs. Konnara Industries wasn't the sort of company I wanted to be working at, I realised. I much prefer where I am now, helping people who need helping and not giving my time to a shale gas company. Come into the living room for a minute… you too, Oscar!" She called his name loudly so he could hear from the bathroom. "We need a 'family chat'!" Mrs Cooper laughed at the corny sound of it.

Ice followed, nonplussed, and sat herself on the arm of the couch, face impassive but thoughts beginning to churn out the possibilities of why the family would need to gather for a talk. Things like this were rarely good news. Mad random ideas came into her head before she dismissed them: divorce, illness, bankruptcy. All the big things that might impact everyone. Ice did not want to believe that any of these were likely.

Mr Cooper and Oscar arrived simultaneously. Her brother plonked himself down next to Ice, giving her a 'What's Going on?' look to which she shrugged and pulled a 'No Idea' face. The two adults sat opposite them on the living room chairs. Ice waited. She had worked out a while ago that silence was often the best prompt to make people talk. Her dad made a hesitant start.

"We thought we ought to fill you in – let you know what we've been thinking about. If I learned anything last year, Ice, it was that keeping secrets didn't protect you, it just made everything more difficult… and dangerous. Anyway… well you know things aren't great here at the moment. We're surviving, but it doesn't look like the situation is going to improve – in fact the opposite seems likely."

"What do you mean?" Oscar interjected. "What things? What situation?" It was probably his youth that meant Oscar was less likely to notice the changes that were happening around him but Ice was conscious that her father was talking about more than their family situation. There had been changes since they had come to Depton but it was a growing national emergency, not just a local one. She wasn't sure what her parents were going to suggest.

"Well, people are struggling, Oscar." their mother said. We are managing because of my job, but your father still hasn't found any work. There are no places for his engineering skills right now. But it's a bit more serious than that. We think that there's a possibility that difficulties with the food supply will get worse. Don't worry – we have enough for now and we can cope if there are shortages for a while. But eventually, it'll need to get better or people are going to panic again. That's never a good thing. Desperate people do desperate things. We want us to be safe."

At this point there was a pause, as though their parents were allowing the children to process the information. Ice tried to work out what they hadn't yet said but were thinking.

"What are you going to do?" she asked.

"Nothing's planned yet, Ice," her dad replied. "We're just weighing up options." And then he said the words that neither child wanted to hear but knew were coming. "It might involve having to move."

Oscar gave a massive groan and a long, drawn-out, complaining utterance of, "Again?". He leaned his head back against the settee and raised his eyes to the ceiling, sighing heavily. Ice stayed silent. She had kept her cool about moving to Depton, even though it had been annoying starting again with the discomfort of unfamiliar social settings. Against the odds, she had made connections here. There were Mia and Daniel, her friends from her year group who had both helped her out in so many ways – she realised how much she valued their company now – and there was Mrs Bennett, and little Nathan who shared her ability to see the shadelings. She thought of Joe, too, with an unsettling feeling that was hard to interpret. Unlike her younger brother, Ice remained outwardly impassive, true to her name, but she understood and shared his negative reaction.

"Nothing's certain, yet," Mr Cooper said. "But if we need to go, it might be quite sudden. In times like these it pays to be prepared."

"Prepared, how?" Ice asked, imagining suitcases packed by the door and them fleeing into the night.

"Well – think about the things you'd want to take and perhaps we should start slim-lining the stuff we don't need," was their dad's reply.

Both parents were talking calmly, as though these were normal occurrences, but Ice knew that they were covering something deeper. Her parents were genuinely frightened and that scared her.

Mia was late to school the next day. Just as Ice was wondering if her friend was ill, she arrived and slid into the seat next to her. It was immediately apparent that something was wrong. Mia was the most positive person she knew. It had been her genuine smile of welcome that had made Ice's first day a little more bearable all those months ago and if they had to leave Depton, Ice would really miss this kind, funny friend. She leaned over to say, "Hi" but there was no response from her companion. Instead, Mia looked down at the desk so that her shoulder-length, black hair fell forward and obscured her face from view.

"What's wrong?" Ice said, leaning forward to try to make eye-contact. Mia did not answer but shook her head and Ice could see, to her dismay, that Mia's eyes were clouded with tears that proceeded to fall unchecked on to the wooden desk.

"Mi! What is it?" she reiterated, worried now and awkward in the face of human emotion. Mia did not answer. She shrugged off Ice's tentative arm round the shoulder and ran out of the room leaving Ice stunned and immobile.

"I don't know either," came a voice from behind Ice as she was leaving the room, unsure whether to search for her friend or to go to the first lesson of the day. School lessons seemed increasingly irrelevant, but the adults were attempting to maintain routines for the sake of the children and Ice appreciated that. Daniel caught up with her. He was frowning and he shrugged his shoulders in a gesture of puzzlement.

"She didn't seem to want to talk to anybody, though," he continued. "Maybe we need to give her some space and speak at lunch-time."

Ice agreed. She tried to imagine what she, herself, would have wanted. In the old days, before Depton, she was a great master of all her emotions. Ice – cool about everything. But it had been hard to be cool last year. She hadn't been able to isolate herself to avoid uncomfortable interactions like she normally did. The situation had forced her to communicate with people. It had been worth the effort because they had helped her and she had ended up with some close friends.

At lunch-time in the canteen, Mia was nowhere to be seen, but Ice had an inkling where she might be. The school had an enclosure with two pygmy goats, Peaches and Cream, which had become a kind of impromptu meeting place since Ice had joined. The little mammals gave the comfort of uncomplicated animal feelings. They only judged you on whether you had come with treats or not. When Ice got to the fence, she saw that Daniel had beaten her to it. Mia was kneeling down, fingers through one of the gaps in the chicken wire so that she could scratch the head of Peaches who had come to see what was on offer. Daniel was next to her, hands on knees and bent over to talk. Mia's reaction was totally unexpected and out of character. As Daniel reached out a hand to Mia's shoulder, she stood up and shouted, "Just leave me alone!" pushing past Ice on her hurried way back into the school building.

"What the hell was that? What did I do?" Daniel seemed as dismayed as Ice. The three of them rarely needed to raise their voices to each other and they had never fallen out.

"It's not what you *did*; it's what you *are*, that's the problem."

Both turned to the newcomer. They were approached by a tall girl with dark hair worn in a single, long plait. Ice could see there was a resemblance to the friend who had just left so abruptly. This girl was older than Mia by a couple of years but she had the same dark, 'manga heroine' eyes, and her strong Birmingham accent confirmed the relationship: Mia's sister.

"What *I* am? What am I? What is this all about, Kiran?" Daniel asked the older girl.

"Hi," Kiran said to the group, with a little wave and then to Daniel, "I'm afraid, what you are is a white boy."

Ice watched the blood drain from Daniel's face, but to his credit, he kept his temper.

"What do you mean by that?" he asked quietly. His voice was under control though Ice could see the anger behind his eyes. She was angry, too. Their friendship took account of all their differences in many ways, but none of them had ever been accused of being the wrong race.

"Calm down," the girl replied. "She's not mad at you. She's upset by something that happened on the way to school. I'm older so I've learned to deal with it, but Mia isn't so used to that sort of thing. She needs to *get* used to it, though, because it's getting worse."

They both understood what she meant. Hostility towards 'outsiders' had definitely increased. It didn't matter if your family had lived in England for five generations, if you were not white, or you spoke with an accent, you were a target for the crime of being 'foreign'. It was another of the uncomfortable developments that came with the election of a government that wanted the people to be 'proud to be British'. It was a narrow view of British and it was nothing to be proud of.

"It was just some idiot boys," Kiran went on. "I could deal with them calling me a Paki and telling me to 'go home'. 'This *is* my home', I said. I told them to get a brain between them.

But they pushed us and Mia dropped her stuff on the ground. She is way more sensitive than me. It really frightened and upset her. She cried all the way to school and kept saying we needed to go somewhere else."

Ice's head spun with mixed emotions. Her instinct for exacting justice was like heat spreading outwards from her core, and this combined with another deeply unpleasant feeling brought on by the thought of her friend leaving Depton. It seemed like events were conspiring to break up her human relationships after all. If she had been there – if she knew who those boys were – she was not sure she could have kept to her vow of no violence. It was just as well she hadn't witnessed it.

Chapter 5 ~ Daniel

Daniel and Ice agreed that they would talk to Mia after school. They wanted to be there when she was leaving and make sure she wasn't on her own going home. This was sooner than expected. Half an hour into the maths lesson, the school secretary came into their classroom and asked the teacher, Miss Rakkar to step into the corridor. Ice could see them having a quiet conversation outside. When she returned, Miss Rakkar looked like she was angry.

"We're to meet in the hall," she said. "Bring all your belongings."

This caused the normal eruption of loud questioning from the children. It was unusual to be summoned to the hall, but when they were, it always meant something significant needed to be shared. The last time it had happened, there had been a trespasser on the premises and several of the teachers' bags had gone missing. Pupils had been given instructions about what to do if they ever saw someone they did not recognise in the grounds. This was funny because in a school that size, there were several people a day that they did not recognise.

It wasn't an intruder this time. To general hoots of pleasure, the head announced that the school was closing early. She went on to explain that finally their water supply had been turned off and they did not know when it would resume. Because of that, it was likely that the school would not reopen until further notice. Sounds of pleasure turned to confused conversations. Some of the pupils were due to do exams that term. The head silenced all questions. An email would be sent out that afternoon. All pupils were to make their way home or contact parents if necessary.

Ice looked round for Mia. Her friend had not joined them in the hall but was sitting disconsolately at the end of one of the lines. As they all rose to leave, Ice hurried over and grabbed her by the arm.

"I know what happened," she said. "I'm so sorry you're having to put up with this rubbish but we want to make sure you're OK. Please walk home with me and Daniel."

Mia shook her head.

"Thanks," she replied, flatly. "I didn't mean to be rude. I'm just not feeling very friendly at the moment. I'm going with my sister." She paused and then gave Ice a weak smile that began to wobble. Before she could start to cry again, Mia said, "I'll be OK. Speak later," and hurried away.

Ice did not like the feeling she was experiencing. She tried to put herself in Mia's position, but her little friend had always been so positive. Though Ice was angry with the racists, she knew that she had never felt what it really was like to be on the receiving end of that kind of abuse. She tried to tell herself that Mia was not rejecting *her*, personally, but she felt a little sick and alone, nevertheless.

It was Daniel who broke into her reverie.

"No luck, then?" he queried.

"No. She's really upset. I don't know what to do. Do you think we should leave her? If they're closing the school, we're not going to see her unless we call round." Ice looked at him for an answer. She knew he probably wouldn't have any more of a solution than she would, but it was a comfort to have someone to share her dismay.

"I'll text her tonight," Daniel said. "Let's meet up somewhere. It's going to be a long, boring holiday on our own."

The pair of them stepped out into the glare of the October afternoon. There were still several hours of sunlight left.

"In fact," Daniel said, "Come round to mine now. We'll see if we can get Mia on a chat together. Unless you have something better to do."

Ice didn't know what Daniel meant by 'better'. She always had things she could do. She still hadn't fully explored the castle that dominated the town and there were two old bookshops that were not normally accessible to her during the week. It felt like he wanted her to accept his offer, though and so she went along with him, in the opposite direction to her house. Daniel was easy company. He did all the talking and didn't seem to notice nor care that she was mostly silent. In addition, he had an open personality and Ice rarely detected any dishonesty. She was growing very fond of her 'team' which disproved the old saying of, 'Two's company, three's a crowd'. His flow of conversation and Ice's internal thoughts were interrupted by the sound of sirens.

"More fires!" Daniel announced as the two children covered their ears and the three red trucks rattled past them. "The drought has made everything a tinderbox" he observed. "As if we haven't got enough problems."

Ice pulled a wry expression and nodded. 'Tinderbox' was a good word for it. It was an archaic device that hadn't been used for centuries but everyone understood it meant full of combustible material and ready to burst into flames at the slightest spark. This was not the first fire of the season and she doubted it would be the last.

"It doesn't look close, does it? I hope they get it under control before it can spread."

"No it looks like it's over by Bale," Daniel replied. There aren't many houses there – it's mostly fenced-off land. Owned by the government or something. I dunno."

Ice stared off into the distance, watching the brownish, mushroom shape of smoke billowing upwards. Around it, smaller cloud-like patterns were just visible.

"There!" Ice shouted at Daniel. "The birds again!" She willed them to coalesce like they had the other day, so that Daniel could see them for himself. At one point, her heart skipped a beat and she thought she could see the beginnings of a definite outline begin to take shape. Not a giant horse this time – something more strung out and serpentine but with a 'head' at one end. Then it dissipated almost as quickly as it had formed and Daniel made no comment, not seeming to have noticed.

"She's not answering the chat call," Daniel told Ice, after several attempts to get a chat link on his phone. "I can see that she's online, but she's not responding. I feel awful. Like I've done something wrong."

Ice wasn't sure what to reply. She was an expert at masking emotion. When others demonstrated theirs openly, she felt bemused and awkward. If they talked, she intuitively knew whether they were being honest or not, but strong feelings were like a tsunami, overwhelming her senses. As a response, she said, "OK," and then, "Try again, later? Unless we go to her house – but maybe she won't want to see us."

***

When they were up in his room, Daniel did try again but without success. He looked down at his phone as though by staring at it, he could make it give him the response he wanted. They were both sitting on his bed and he had tried several times to get Mia to join a chat session.

"Things are shit, Ice," he muttered, without looking up. "How did we do this to ourselves? We're supposed to be so clever!"

Ice pondered for a second, wondering what particular things he meant and who the 'we' were. Their friends? The racist boys? If it was humans in general, she knew that she didn't have any words of comfort to give but she tried anyway.

"We're clever but we're basically still animals, I think." She gave him a weak smile when he looked at her. "We do things because we've evolved to do them. Get resources if we can. Blame 'others'. Look how basic we are when we're thirsty. We don't care about anything else if we can't have a drink. In our heads, we know what we are doing is destroying things but we can't stop. We might be naturally sort of greedy. It's how we survived millions of years ago. To make a difference, everyone needed to overcome their basic nature. That probably was never possible."

Daniel gave a bitter laugh. Putting his arm round Ice's shoulders, he said, "Wow! That was a long speech for you! Depressingly right, probably. So what? Do we just give up?"

Ice thought back to times when she had wanted to give up. What had kept her going was always the details and not the bigger picture.

"I don't know," she replied, feeling awkward under the weight of Daniel's arm still resting across her. "Maybe the whole human race is doomed. Maybe we'll take out all the living things on the planet with us. But we don't stop trying and we don't stop looking after the things we can. We can't save everything, but we never could. All living things come to an end anyway – although not normally all at the same time! What we *can* do is be kind to the individuals that are around us. Like those people in Australia, rescuing the koalas. They knew that they couldn't get to them all, but they still looked after the ones they could save for a little while. Gave them water. Bandaged their burnt paws."

Ice was a little amazed at her own speech. She must have been thinking these things for some time without being fully aware of them. Daniel did not remove his arm from her shoulder, but shifted towards her and moved the other one to join it so that she was sitting stiffly on his bed while squeezed rather tightly in his arms. Ice had learned of the power of a human embrace last year. She had needed it when Mia had thrown her arms around her, making her feel less alone. Now she was unsure how to react to Daniel. His scruffy blond hair was in her face, tickling her cheek, but the warm, boyish scent of it was not unpleasant, so she tentatively put one arm around him in response and patted him on his back as one does to a small child. At this, Daniel laughed out loud and Ice did too, grateful to have briefly broken the mood and the tension.

"We bandage each others' paws!" He held up his two hands, fingers curled over like he was a small animal. So you have a little hope, then – to keep going?" She hesitated before replying, thinking about what it actually meant to have hope. Ice was sure she did not have that. Hope was the cruellest thing because it was always accompanied by fear of disappointment. In the past, what she had felt had been more like determination. Now it was less than that – but still something.

"I don't think it's hope that keeps me going. It's more like curiosity."

"I wish I could be as chilled about it as you."

"I'm *Ice*, remember!" she said with a shrugging spread of her hands.

Chapter 6 ~ Encounter

For the first couple of days out of school, there was a kind of pattern. Ice made the morning tea and sipped it in the kitchen with her father. He was still leaving the house early to talk to people he knew – connections he had made through work – in the hope that someone might want an industrial engineer who was trying his best to keep positive. Every evening he came home deflated but still determined and she wondered how he could carry on. She wondered *how long* he would carry on. She was pretty sure that companies weren't looking for experts in fracking machinery. It was the problem of becoming too specialised. He needed to broaden his search and lower his expectations, but nobody wanted to tell him that.

For Ice, there was a twice-daily dog walk, taken in turns and sometimes with Oscar. She liked the company of the boxer, and of her brother. Both of them had the immediate approach to life of animals and young children, whether it was burying one's nose in an interesting smell or burying one's nose in a virtual world. They didn't dwell on the past, nor anticipate the future much beyond their next meal.

The daily drudge of obtaining food and waiting for the water to come on had almost become normal and people seemed to accept that they had to queue for basic items. These days they grumbled and sometimes showed their annoyance by swearing when things ran out, but after the earlier panic buying and some violent incidents across the country, they had managed to return to some degree of civility and there had even been acts of kindness and support. Brawling in the streets was not yet a feature of this small Midlands town.

Everyone was waiting for things to get back to normal but deep down they feared, or perhaps knew, that would not happen. Some people, like Anna King, Daniel's mum, argued that things should not go back to normal because that was the problem in the first place.

Since Ice had come to Depton, she had become a lot more aware of issues in the real world and much less absorbed in exploring the past. She knew that the evidence her mother had found was damning. The fracking company, Konnara Industries, where both her parents had worked, had tried to cover up the risks to the local area and there had been bribery so that drilling could go ahead anyway. But that was just a tiny part of it. The wider destruction of the environment ran deep and it was hard to ignore the change in the weather. People had shifted their denial. Not many continued to argue that it was not happening or that it was not caused by human activity. Now a kind of fatalism had set in: it was too late and there was nothing to be done about it.

Ice sighed. Her mother would be giving evidence right at this moment. She so wanted it to go well. The case against Konnara was helped by the fact that Nathan Bennett's father was the County Councillor named in the report. He had let the company play down the risks and pushed for permission to let them drill. Ice remembered the video Anna King had shown her of Mr Bennett and one of the Konnara directors on the news saying how good the drilling would be for the local economy. Unfortunately, evidence showed that he had taken some sizeable 'donations' from the company. Bribes, really. Ice's mother had documents and emails that the police had taken seriously, at last. But when Councillor Bennett's own son had gone missing, Ice had found him and Mr Bennett had

had a fit of gratitude – or guilt – and he had admitted everything. That hadn't stopped the company doing whatever it could to try to cover its tracks, though. Communications from Konnara's lawyers to Ice's mother had become quite alarming and threatening. She had resigned, but she had not backed down.

Ice was alone with Buddy in the house. She relished these times. Small sounds were amplified in the near silence. She sat at the kitchen table and listened to the gentle snores from his bed in the corner of the room. Occasionally there would be a creak from the house as something expanded in the growing heat of the morning. Traffic noises were just audible but not as frequent as they would have been a couple of years ago. Sensibly, people saved their fuel ration for times when they needed to make a journey. Everyone was supposed to have transitioned to electric cars by now, but many could not afford to and had hung on to their ten-year old petrol models instead.

It was good to hear the sparrows shouting at each other. A family of them had thrived in the thorny hedge. All signs of animal activity were welcome. Ice wondered whether the otters were coping with the drought. She had only caught sight of them once, very briefly last year when she was walking Buddy by the river. She'd heard the telltale plopping sound, and two smooth, brown backs had arched through the surface of the water and disappeared below. Then a small dog-like head had emerged further upstream and cut a gentle wake before dipping back down. Ice's breath had caught in her throat. They had reminded her so much of the shadelings. She had not seen either the shadelings nor the otters since, though she continued to look out for both.

The 'ping' of a message came from the tablet that was resting in front of her, and cut through her meandering thoughts. It was Mia.

soz for being such a bap

Ice allowed herself a small grin. The tone of the message was a good sign. She wanted Mia back to her cheerful self. She was sure Daniel would be relieved too. Their young friend had avoided seeing them both since school had broken up, but she had eventually started texting. In her reply now, Ice suggested meeting up in the park – she'd bring Buddy. She was quite prepared for Mia to try to wriggle out of it, so was pleasantly surprised when she agreed.

"Come on, Bud. Go *out?*" she said to the sleeping dog, once she had put on her shoes.

The emphasis on the word 'out' was Buddy's trigger. He snapped out of his dog dreams, eyes suddenly wide and alert, and jumped up from the bed, making Ice laugh out loud at his eagerness.

Mia seemed glad to see them both and Buddy did his normal wiggling greeting for people he knew. Then Ice let him off the lead and the two girls walked behind, following his excited scamper. The park had been allowed to become parched and the usual beds of town flowers now held just brown, dusty remnants and hardier weeds that were more resilient to the weather. These had taken advantage of the lack of human interference and grew in straggly clumps. Buddy investigated and irrigated them, along with every other significant spot next to the path – catching up on his 'pee-mails' according to Oscar.

"How are you liking our time off?" Ice asked, breaking the silence as they strolled.

"It's OK. A sort of long half term going into Christmas," Mia replied. "I seem to be doing a lot of drawing!" She turned to Ice and gave her a quick smile. "You OK?"

Ice pondered this for a moment, thinking about the 'family chat' that had happened the other night. Nothing more had been said about it since, but the idea of it had lingered, like a threat, and all the family had been subdued with each other since. Oscar was almost completely engrossed in online games. Ice reflected with a pang, that it had been several days since she had said more than a few words to her little brother.

"My parents were talking about maybe needing to leave Depton."

Mia nodded and looked at the ground.

"Mine too," she said, pulling a pout which was a deliberately silly exaggeration to cover strong feelings. "It's almost certain we will, actually. My dad says it might be safer if we go to his relatives. With it being a bit tricky here and you know - like that thing that happened..." Her voice tailed off. Ice could tell that Mia was embarrassed. She scowled. Her friend was the victim. The racists should have been ashamed — not her. But Mia's words had revived that uncomfortable feeling in the pit of her stomach. If her family were also talking about leaving, it gave the whole idea more weight.

"Aren't things quite hard in India, with the heat now though?" Ice asked. "Have you got somewhere to live there?"

"No – we wouldn't go to India. Yes, you're right – we can't live there. They've all gone. My family there. The ones who could afford to. They left last year and moved all the way north to somewhere in Russia."

"Russia!" It seemed an odd choice. Did people go to Russia? In the past, old people had retired to places like Spain and Portugal. Her own grandparents, her mother's parents whom she had never met, had sent polite emails showing pictures of the Algarve until it had become too hot and they had moved back to their native Ireland. She didn't think Russia was all that welcoming to immigrants, but maybe things had changed with their new president.

"Yeah. They want people there now, apparently. My uncle is an expert in renewable energy. They're turning some of the north into massive wind-farms, I think. That part that used to be really cold – well it's warmer now I suppose. I presume it's still windy! Anyway, the flooding has also been bad where my family live in India. They don't really have much choice."

The two girls fell silent after this. It looked like a distinct possibility that either or both would be leaving Depton. For now, though, they had the freedom of the town and no school until further notice.

"We should give Daniel a call and go up the common," she said, suddenly. Things are a bit dry, but the woods are still nice.

***

It was great to have the three of them back together. They didn't need to do anything very special, and even though Mia and Daniel had been friends before Ice had arrived, nobody seemed to resent each other or feel like they were being left out. Perhaps it was because none of them, least of all Ice, sought attention. She was quite happy for Daniel and Mia to chat, while the three of them made seats of the dry cylindrical pieces of trunk from a great tree that had been felled.

The forest was quiet and dappled dark, but small hoverflies still stalked their territory, miraculously holding themselves in the air as though suspended by invisible strings in each patch of sunlight. Buddy lay stretched out in the closest thing he could find to shade, utterly relaxed apart from the occasional twitch of his paw giving away some happy dream. Mia was laughing again too. Daniel had that way with him. Cheeky enough to be charming, but deeply kind and with a quick, silly wit that meant he could turn everything on its head with phrase or a single pun. Ice observed them together. They were like the physical opposites of each other: the boy, tall and blond – Viking genes, maybe; the girl, small, dark, dead straight hair that always looked just brushed, in contrast to Ice's own scruffy waves. Daniel had been Mia's 'mentor' when she had arrived at Depton High, just as Mia had been Ice's. And so the baton of friendship was passed one to the other. Was this really going to be it? Were they all going to be spread about the world soon?

Ice deflected the thought. She knew by now that the most carefully-crafted plans could be scuppered in an instant. All it took was one event. An earthquake. A flood. A drought. War. Homes were washed away, people lost their jobs or their lives. Nothing was certain or permanent.

She caught a sideways glance from Daniel. He was laughing, but for a second there was something else. It was only a slight shift, but a momentary intensity she hadn't noticed before. He looked startled to catch her eye and then dropped his gaze to the ground.

"Hey," he said, standing quickly and brushing off the dried moss from the seat of his trousers. "Look at the time. We should probably get going."

Through the branches, Ice could see that the shadows had grown longer. It was late afternoon. The three of them stepped out from the wood into an open field of brown grass that had once been a golf course. Between the dry stems, the sandy bunkers could be seen but the place was unkempt and had lost its former function years ago. Ice preferred it this way. Nature could take over quickly if unchecked by human activity and although now dry, there was plenty of evidence that plants had flourished in the previous rains.

The course was a favourite of dog walkers and Buddy was leading like he normally did, but unusually, there were no other people around. Their route took them through the open area, some two hundred metres across, towards a stile at the far end with a fence and row of trees that separated them from the road. Between the trunks, the sun shone low in the sky, still bright and intense, causing them to shade their eyes and squint.

Halfway to the stile, Ice stopped and grabbed Buddy by the collar, pulling up the other two who were with her. She put her finger to her lips in a command of silence and indicated a wide patch of longer grass near the fence. The others followed her stare and her pointing finger. Something rustled the grass. A shape moved. Buddy gave a rumbling growl and Ice had to clip on the lead and wrap it several times round her wrist to stop him running forwards. There was an ear visible and then the tip of a flicking tail. As casually as if it were a leopard on an African plain, a large black cat rose from where it had been lying, lazily stretched out a back leg and turned towards them, returning their stares. Then it opened its mouth in a wide yawn so that they could see huge, white incisors, before it sauntered

off in the fluid, soundless manner of panthers, and leaped
into the darkness of the trees.

<h1 align="center">Chapter 7 ~ Lorry</h1>

"**W**as that a *cat?*" Daniel asked. His tone was incredulous, giving away that he knew very well it wasn't just an everyday pet.

"It was enormous wasn't it?" Mia said. "*Wasn't* it? Not just a trick of the light, or..." she laughed, "heatstroke or something. It can't have been a domestic moggy. A *huge* cat. Like a proper big one! My heart rate just went up several notches. Did you see those teeth?"

Ice was glad they had all witnessed it. For once it hadn't just been her seeing strange creatures. This one had been hard to miss. A large cat – certainly much bigger than a normal tabby – had nonchalantly crossed their path and slunk into the undergrowth where it had seemingly vanished. She nodded.

"No, that was definitely not somebody's kitty," she replied. "Unless they were keeping a panther! Maybe it escaped from somewhere. A zoo? Or somebody dumped it, poor thing. If people are leaving their dogs, then it wouldn't surprise me if a large predator was too much to look after." She wasn't sure. What was it with all these giant creatures? Only this one was definitely real and not a flock of birds!

"Well it seems to be doing OK. It didn't look hungry – lucky for us!" Daniel said. He put his arms around the shoulders of the girls on either side of him and gave them a rough rub up and down as if to dispel the adrenaline. "Damn! I was stupid to not get a video of it on my phone. Idiot! But I was frozen to the spot! Do you think we should report it?"

"No!" Ice replied quickly. "No, leave it. It's fine isn't it? They'll only kill it if we tell anyone."

"OK, I'm cool with that," Daniel replied. "Let's get on the road. But quickly. I don't fancy becoming the next meal of an exotic wild animal."

The incident had left the four of them, Buddy included, in a state of heightened excitement as they walked along the roadside. Mia, especially seemed to be chattering a lot and on the verge of giggles. She had her phone out and was snapping selfies and pictures of things along the way, determined not to miss another shot of a big cat, should it emerge from the hedgerow. It was a great contrast to her recent sad mood and Ice welcomed it, even if it was mainly the expression of nervous energy.

They had come out of the common on the opposite side to town where it was bordered by a road without a pavement. It was one of the routes that led just past Depton through the Warwickshire countryside. There was only a narrow, dusty verge where they walked between the roadside and the trees and bushes. Daniel kept glancing into the evergreens that had kept some of their dense foliage and joked with the girls that they needed to be careful in case any large predators were lurking there.

"Yeah. While you're looking for big cats, make sure you don't get run over by any big cars!" Mia retorted. There wasn't much traffic on the road, but it was intimidating to be buzzed by those that were driving too fast and too close. It might have been better to have turned back and gone the way they came but they were committed to this route now and more than half way.

They heard the low rumble of the heavy vehicles before they saw them. The four walkers pressed themselves back against the hedge as the first lorry roared past them, the driver seemingly unaware of the pedestrians on the roadside. It was a bulky vehicle with a dark grey cab pulling a plain white, unmarked tank of the kind Ice had seen sometimes at petrol stations. It looked an oversized juggernaut on the small Warwickshire road. Ice was aware that Daniel was pointlessly shouting in anger, "Hey! Watch out, you bandit! Bloody idiot!"

Buddy began a volley of noisy barks as another and then another of the great vehicles came in succession. Ice could hear Mia utter, "Oh my God!" right at the point where the third lorry appeared round the corner, taking up more than half the road. From the opposite direction a tractor had just pulled out of its field and there was nowhere for the lorry to pass and no way for the driver to stop in time. They stared in horror from their side of the road as the tanker swerved across the opposite lane, missing the tractor but careering into the hedge. Trying to correct the movement and regain the tarmac, the driver swung the cab round to his left, oversteering in his panic. Instead of bringing it back under control, he caused the tank to be catapulted round with the momentum, dragging the whole vehicle over and ripping out the hedgerow, before it came to a crashing halt in a cloud of dust.

It was true that time gave the appearance of slowing in moments of intensity. The whole sequence could only have lasted a few seconds from start to finish, but Ice felt as though she and the others were rooted to the spot for ages, watching the action in slow motion and in great detail. Specific things were highlighted for her in strange ways: the farmer's look of astonishment fixed on his face throughout; the sound of whale-song which she realised afterwards was the scraping of metal on metal; the way one of the great wheels continued to spin after everything had come to a stop.

While the dust was still settling, the farmer jumped down from the tractor and ran to the cab that was resting on its side, just off the road. Daniel was the first of the three spectators to come to his senses and quickly joined him, the pair of them pulling open the cab door against the force of gravity, and helping the stunned driver to clamber out. By now, Buddy was going frantic with excitement. He was rarely frightened – he was the only dog Ice knew that would happily watch fireworks – but surprises always made him bark. Ice held him tightly on the short-wound lead and crouched down, gripping him gently by the scruff to calm him.

"We should phone 999," Mia said, eventually. There was a tremor in her voice, but she was already tapping out the number on her phone. Ice nodded. She could see that the driver of the lorry had walked with the farmer and Daniel some distance away from the tanker. With a jolt of alarm, Ice thought of those times she had seen in movies where crashes like this had burst into flames or exploded. She and Mia needed to get out of the blast zone. She took hold of Mia's arm and her friend allowed herself to be pulled away while still talking to someone on the phone, giving location and situation details. As they began to move to a safer distance, Ice saw the lorry driver shaking his head and remonstrating with the farmer. She could not hear what he was saying, but noticed the farmer take his phone from his shirt pocket and the driver reach out a hand to stop him. Then he appeared to be brushing off the obvious attempts by his rescuers to persuade him not to return to the cab. The farmer gave an exasperated shrug of his shoulders and climbed back on the tractor. He leaned over and said something to Daniel, who stepped up on to a metal platform on the side and held on to a vertical rail, hitching a ride to where the girls stood.

"Are you girls OK?" the farmer asked as Daniel jumped down and joined them. They nodded.

"Is the driver uninjured?" Ice replied. "We've phoned 999. Do we need to do anything else? Like stay till they arrive or something?"

The tractor driver was much younger than Ice had thought, when seeing him from a distance. His hair was cropped short and he had allowed a small amount of juvenile stubble to grow on his face. Early twenties maybe. Perhaps he was only a farm hand or agricultural college student, she mused. He shrugged again and seemed annoyed. There was a slight tremor in his voice when he spoke, testament to his near miss.

"The guy doesn't appear to want our help. He said he had it all under control and that he would sort it out. It's clear of the road, anyway. Apparently he was phoning the company or whoever – and the recovery people. It looks a write-off to me. But I don't see what else we can do now, so if you're all OK, I'd rather not hang around. I need to get on."

"Won't the police need us to stay and give statements or something?" Ice asked. "Will they be long?"

"Don't know," he replied. "If they need me, they can find me through the farm. But I doubt it. And to be honest, I could do without the hassle. It's hard enough these days." He didn't wait for their response and for a little while, without speaking, they watched the tractor continue to make its slow progress down the road. Somewhat unsure that they should be leaving the scene, but not knowing what else to do, the three silently agreed that they ought to get back to Depton before the light had gone completely.

"I got all of that," Mia announced, holding up her phone as they walked. They turned, wide-eyed. "I'll send it to you both," she continued.

"Well done!" Daniel exclaimed. "You did better than me! That could be useful evidence, maybe, if the police get in touch with you again. They probably will, you know, because you were the one that made the call." He winced and bent down, examining the skin on his right calf.

"Ouch! What have you done to yourself, Dan?" Ice pulled a grimace. Daniel had on the faded grey, knee-length shorts which he had favoured most of the summer and she could see that somehow he had managed to acquire a four-inch gash to his lower leg. It was trickling dark, red blood into his shoe.

"I hadn't noticed it before," he replied. "But ow!" He pulled a mock sad face and gave the girls his 'puppy dog' eyes, as if fishing for sympathy. "I slipped down there when I went to help. Must have cut it on a bit of sharp metal where the side of the tanker had ripped open."

Chapter 8 ~ Deletion

Mia sent the video later that evening. It was incredible to watch what happened again in real time. She had begun to film at the point where the second vehicle had passed them on the road, perhaps thinking that she could post it on social media later with a complaint about irresponsible drivers and the companies that employed them. Ice could see where the tank had been ripped and where Daniel slipped, though from the angle of the shot, she had to guess that it was where he had cut his leg open. The images were small on the phone screen, but she could tell that once the driver had been 'rescued', he seemed more concerned about his lorry than his own safety. Mia's video ended with a shot of the young farmer driving away down the road.

Technology was so handy sometimes. When Ice's mother returned home from the court, much later than expected, Ice had already shown the video to her father and to Oscar, so they knew exactly why the route Mrs Cooper would have taken had been blocked off and why she had had to go the longer way round back to Depton. Ice handed her the phone as explanation and the video was played again while the others looked on for her reaction.

"Yes. This will be it!" she exclaimed. "You children were there? What were you doing? Is everyone OK?"

"We're all fine," Ice replied. "Even the lorry driver is fine. We were on the way home from the common. Daniel accidentally cut his leg, but it's only a flesh wound, as they say. It was all very dramatic but nobody got badly hurt. I suppose that the road was blocked while they got the lorry back up and towed."

Ice's mum stared at the phone screen without speaking for a moment.

"I got turned away at the top of the road, by the main junction," she said. "I could see something was going on, but it looked like a much bigger operation than just clearing a lorry. They had hazard-taped the roadway and there were lots of people standing on the other side. I could have sworn two of them were armed! Some of them were wearing those white protective suits – you know, the 'hazmat' type ones. I presumed there was some kind of investigation – like they'd found a body or something, because there were also those white tents that they put up round crime scenes."

"Weird!" Oscar interjected. He had the typical 10-year-old's fascination for drama, even though most of it was the kind that played out on his mobile phone in some virtual world. "Mia should upload that video. Or better, she should sell it to someone. Like Flicweb. Maybe she already did and it'll be on the local news. Hey – it'll be on there anyway won't it? And we can see why there was all that big operation. Cool!"

They did watch for the news that night. They also searched the Internet for posts about the accident but there was no mention of it. Ice's father suggested that it was probably just too early for an event like that to have made itself on to the news. They might have all agreed with this had Oscar not nagged Ice to contact Mia again and suggest she upload the video to their social media page. At least then, he said, it would get 'hits' and be picked up by the news channels, maybe. But when Ice phoned Mia, she was told that the video had gone.

"What do you mean, 'gone'?" she asked her friend. "Did you accidentally delete it? How did you manage that? Anyway,

I'm sure that you can get it back from the cloud backup – can't you?"

"I've tried," Mia said. "It's not on there. I can't find it. You've got it though, haven't you? Can you send it to me?"

Ice clicked on Mia's name in her messenger. Everything they had sent to each other in the last six months would still be on her phone. Except that it wasn't. Mia was still in her friends list, but the message box was completely blank. It was as though she had never received a single text. When they checked with Daniel, they discovered that the same thing had happened to his phone. Somehow the messages from Mia had all been deleted and there was no backup of those, nor the video in the cloud.

Chapter 9 ~ Beasts

The incident with the video disappearing was very unsettling, particularly when Ice shared that information with her parents and they had seemed concerned rather than dismissive. They hadn't told her to not worry and that it was all probably a technical glitch. Instead, her mother had said, "That *is* rather odd," and then both parents had closed themselves in the study where they held a muted conversation that Ice could not quite hear through the door.

Combined with her mother's story about what she had seen on the road, it was a bit sinister. Ice did not like thinking that her phone had been hacked or that unknown people were looking at her personal messages and information. She had her phone password-protected and used the usual software that was supposed to stop malware and identity theft, but apparently it hadn't worked. All apps had cloud-based memory these days and it looked like someone, for some reason, had deleted the crash video. But why would anyone want to do that? What was it about the things that she and her friends had seen that would lead to a 'cover-up' if that's what this was? She began to feel a little scared for Mia. She was the one who had left the message for the emergency services. Was there any reason she wouldn't be safe?

Ice put the thought from her head – it was verging on paranoid conspiracy theories. Sometimes the Internet could be glitchy. Things did get deleted occasionally. Computer viruses could do that. Perhaps they had inadvertently picked one up. She concentrated, instead, on the plan for the day. She was alone in the house again. Oscar and her father had taken Buddy out and her mother was at work. Ice remembered she still had the book that had helped her in the spring of the previous year, when she had seen the creepy, little creatures in the town. It was called 'The Depton Shadelings and Other Myths of the Midlands'. She had grown rather fond of the shadelings in the end. Ice rather wished they were around, now. But they were only one of many myths that the author of the book had included and she was sure she remembered something that related to what they'd seen the previous day – and also to her own weird sightings of the mysterious flocks of birds that seemed to transform into other things.

There was a chapter on the Dun Cow of Warwickshire, and Ice couldn't suppress a quick snort of laughter thinking back to Oscar's silly impression of it mooing madly with rolling eyes. The cow was said to be huge – many times the size of a normal cow – and could supply milk to everyone who asked. One day it had been angered and gone on the rampage, finally being killed by Guy of Warwick.

"Of course!" Ice thought to herself, bitterly. She felt indignant and sorry for the cow, even though it was only a mythical beast. "Of course, they'd kill it. What else? Poor Dun Cow!" It had left its name to many pubs in the county, though. The information in the final paragraph was what caught her eye, however. She was right! The author described the cow as possibly belonging to a wider set of huge, mythical creatures from the area, many of which it seemed had fallen victim to Guy's slaughtering tendencies. There had been a giant boar and even a dragon! Ice wondered how much of his reputation Guy of Warwick had forged himself and how much was embellishment over time. A dragon might seem far-fetched if she hadn't seen supposedly mythological creatures for real. There were the shadelings, and now the strange bird-flock creatures. Could they be the huge beasts of the folklore? Nobody else had even seen them and she began to doubt herself. Maybe they were just very convincing but natural patterns.

Ice mentally shrugged and scanned the chapter headings. It was so obvious, she couldn't believe she hadn't remembered and thought of it at the time. The title of the chapter jumped out at her and she gave herself a private reprimand for not having paid more attention to the rest of the book when she had read it before. Giving herself an imaginary face-palm, Ice read the title: 'The Beast of Bale'. Bale! It was only just up the road. And the beast! It was a more recent legend: a large cat, seen near Bale, some twenty years ago. There had been some sightings and people had found footprints. Unsurprisingly and as usual, there was no proof that it existed, apart from a very grainy video of some kind of animal, dark and blurry, at the far end of a wheat-field. It might easily have been a domestic cat or a fake. It didn't matter. It was pretty clear to Ice that what she and her friends had seen was just like the description of 'The Beast of Bale'. Only it couldn't have been the same one unless it had an extraordinarily long life-span.

Had things ever been normal and straightforward? Ice wondered to herself. Did other people lead lives which were filled with supernatural creatures and weird events? In answer to her own question she decided that they probably did not. For some reason most people didn't notice the things she did. But now they were all living in a time that was no longer 'normal'. Or at least it felt like things had changed since she was very young and more so since before, when her parents were children.

Perhaps 'normal' was just what people got used to. In the Middle Ages, the Black Death was normal. During World War Two, it was normal to sleep between the tracks in the underground while the enemy dropped bombs on your city. Some things were not noticeable until there was a dramatic change. 'Boiling a Frog' was the unpleasant expression that was used, meaning that if you changed the temperature of the water gradually, the poor frog wouldn't realise it was being boiled until it was too late. Ice didn't believe this cruel expression would be true for the frogs. They were sensitive creatures. What it really meant was that people would not notice something bad was happening if each step was a small, imperceptible one one. Climate, for example. The scientists had been trying to warn people for decades about the impact of heating up the Earth but many had been unable to grasp the reality of it – to absorb the fact that it would change their lives. Even now, there were still those who carried on as though it was just 'freak weather' and made plans for the future that would most likely be impossible. It was obvious to anyone who paid attention, that the successive floods and droughts were not just the odd occurrence. The whole pattern had shifted.

Some things changed more rapidly. Supply issues had cut off people's access to basic necessities overnight. That hadn't been a slow unnoticeable creep. One day, there were supermarkets full of everything people wanted and the next day the shelves were empty. They had never refilled properly.

Ice suppressed the slight rise in panic that thoughts like these brought. It was important to deal with things and carry on. Some events might be fairly predicable, but nobody could really tell the future.

"Unless you are a witch!" Ice thought wryly. That conjured the thought of the strange woman from the stone circle. Apparently *she* could predict what was going to happen, though it had been the usual vague foretelling of doom and gloom. Even more doom and gloom? Ice tried to recall what she had read about Samhain. She knew enough to know what the woman meant, though she pronounced it, 'sowwin'. She had said that it was approaching, which was right enough. As far as Ice could remember it was something to do with Halloween, but an old festival. One of the ancient, pagan ones that had been hijacked by the Christian Church so that the local people wouldn't feel hard-done-by for losing their traditions.

Ice still had the old computer she had set up on the desk by her bedroom window. She moved to this now and sat down, turning it on with a click and waiting for it to boot up. It did connect to the Internet, though some websites no longer functioned on the old operating system. It was good enough for most of Ice's purposes. She enjoyed the use of the proper keyboard, and the large screen made searching for things easy, but her phone was handy, in case she needed it.

She read the text displayed on the site she had brought up with her search:

> Samhain is a Celtic festival occurring at the end of the month of October about halfway between the autumn equinox (days and nights of equal length), and the winter solstice (the shortest day). It is thought to date back as far as neolithic times and was the day when the cattle were brought in and animals slaughtered for the winter. Samhain is considered a time when boundaries between our

world and the 'other world' are dissolved and more easily crossed, allowing travel by supernatural creatures, spirits and pagan gods. Offerings of food and drink are left outside for the ghosts of dead relatives who can visit at this time. 'Halloween' owes its origins to this festival. Modern Wiccans and Pagans have revived the celebration of the old festival and consider it a religious holiday.

There had been a fair amount of 'boundary crossing' in Depton already, Ice thought to herself, but the text helped her to make more sense of the witch woman's warnings. She had spoken about the 'old spirits' and the 'fabric of the world growing thin'. Ice would have liked to dismiss it as the ravings of an old hippy, but she couldn't. The woman had known that Ice had seen things – otherworldly creatures. The myths about huge animals, the woman's warnings, the history of Samhain – they all fitted together – with each other and with the giant, black beasts she had seen created by the flocks of birds. The shadelings had revealed important things she would not otherwise have known, but if the great beasts were showing her something, she had no idea what it was.

Chapter 10 ~ Joe

Days without structure could lose their routine and identity. What did it matter what day of the week it was when you weren't forced to get up and go out for anything in particular? Ice felt empathy for her father, still out of work and supposedly looking for another job but beginning to spend more time in his 'office' doing things that weren't necessarily very productive. She still woke early and took him his cup of tea, but he had stopped going out every day.

The Internet was a time-killer. You could start by thinking that you were going to do some research or look for companies that were employing engineers, and end up down the rabbit hole of strange news stories and videos of funny animals. Sometimes he would emerge and complain that the day had gone by without him noticing or achieving anything much.

Not wanting to fall into the same trap, Ice had given herself some routine for the week. She missed the school day, the taught content, such as it was, and the imposed deadlines. She knew that if she wasn't careful she would end up bored and drifting. Buddy provided a good reason to get out at least twice, which she did sometimes on foot and sometimes on the bike. He still had the stamina of a young dog and was normally quite happy to exercise for as long as possible, but because of the heat of the day, it tended to be first thing and in the late evening. For the in-between times, she had made herself a basic schedule: reading for research; at least one boring household chore; something creative like drawing or writing; some indolence like sitting in the garden or watching the telly. In addition to the daily timetable, Ice had also added those things to her calendar that she promised herself she would do. They mainly involved exploring the local sites of interest. There were still many parts of the area that she had yet to visit.

Designing this routine and typing it up on the computer felt good. Of course she didn't have to stick to it, but she liked the knowledge that she wasn't going to sit around wondering what to do, or, like her father, burn up the hours on distraction activities. She had also taken on the role of supermarket queueing once a week, when rations were in.

Two days after the lorry incident, she stood in one of these, in the morning heat, hugging the shade on the pavement outside the shop, waiting with the other residents of Depton as the queue made its slow progress inside. Shopping in the old days had been a different activity to what it was now. Then, you could wander about and browse the shelves, putting whatever you wanted into your trolley. Goods came from far away places. She remembered marvelling at plastic-wrapped trays of blackberries from Mexico. It seemed mad, given that blackberries grew as weeds in the rough ground behind the store and you could pick them for free! Now it was a much more regimented operation. Everyone had to have the ration app on their phone if they wanted to get groceries. You still had to pay, of course, but it was meant to stop bulk-buying and make it fairer for all. It was common knowledge, however, that you could get whatever you wanted if you had enough money. The rich could find a way round most restrictions.

Thoughts like these occupied Ice's mind whilst she watched the others in the queue. It was mainly women, interestingly enough. Was that because the men felt it was beneath them, or were women just the natural foragers? Perhaps this was the

21st Century equivalent of picking berries and digging roots. Ice felt that she would have actually preferred to do those things than queue for supermarket rations.

A woman's voice came from behind her in the queue, saying her name and asking her how she was. Ice turned to see Anna King, Daniel's mother and gave her a wry smile. She shrugged, puffing air from her lips in a way that indicated that she was fine, all things considered, but with the unspoken agreement that queueing for food wasn't what either of them would prefer to be doing.

"I'm well, thanks," she replied, nodding. "We're all surviving." There was a pause while she wondered if she was expected to continue the conversation and whether she should talk about the other members of her family. "Are you all OK?" she asked.

"Yes – we're alright, I suppose," Mrs King answered. "Daniel needed a couple of stitches in his leg, but it's healing. He's been a bit poorly, actually. Coming down with an autumn virus, I expect. Typical to get it just as he has all this freedom! He probably picked it up from school, right before it closed."

Ice realised with a sudden pang of guilt that she hadn't spoken to Daniel since the video footage had been erased from her phone. She was a little ashamed to have not checked on either of her friends. The phone hacking had unnerved her and she had tried to think about other things instead – but using it to communicate felt unsafe. She wasn't sure if Mrs King knew about it, and was considering asking her – she would have welcomed her thoughts. She was halfway through saying that she hoped Daniel's bug was a short one, when her attention was taken by the shop assistant at the distribution counter and so, instead they both nodded their 'goodbyes' and split off to the available positions.

The set-up reminded Ice of an old bank rather than a supermarket. It was quite a good system, really. On the phone app, the customer chose the items they wanted from their rations and then at the supermarket entrance, these were scanned by the system. When the goods reached the distribution counter, your number was flashed on the screen and the items were ready to be taken already deducted on the app. Even the little old ladies in the queue had managed to make it work, though some of them still paid in old, physical money. A lot of people used cards at the checkout. Others, like Ice had bank details linked to the app itself and the money was transferred automatically. It wasn't even real money, she thought, moving the purchases from the counter into her rucksack. It was just a load of pieces of information in a computer – electronic code that made one set of numbers go up and another set go down. It was very sophisticated – the latest way of conducting trade. And yet, ironically, in the 'real world' more and more people were being forced to do things by the oldest known traditions: bartering items that they needed; exchanging services directly for goods in the ways humans had done thousands of years ago. The newest and the oldest modes operating side by side.

Ice swung the rucksack on to her back. It was disappointingly light but at least they had some good basics in the store. She'd managed to get another fair-sized block of cheese and some autumn vegetables that had survived the drought. As she fastened the clip at the front and began to make her way along the route to the shop exit, she noticed Joe at one of the distribution points ahead of her. He had not seen her and seemed to be involved in some kind of argument with the shop assistant.

"Look, that can't be right! Can you just check again?". Joe was speaking quietly but his voice had an urgent, desperate edge with none of his customary cheekiness. The shop assistant was shaking her head and beginning to move the groceries below the counter again. Ice was surprised to see Joe grab one of the items and try to tug it back. Other customers in the shop had begun to notice the commotion and were looking at them with that bemused interest people have when something slightly unpleasant is happening to someone else. She heard a deep voice behind her say, "Excuse me, please," and she quickly stepped out of the way as a man pushed past to get to where Joe was standing. It was obvious that things were escalating. The man's jacket was an official type: blue with reflective strips and emblazoned with the word, 'security' on the back.

"Don't touch me!" Joe shouted, wrenching himself away from the security guard's hands. "I'm just getting my stuff, like everyone else! Those are my rations!" He pointed to the things that were still on the counter. "And the ones she's put under! Give them back!" Both the pitch and the volume of his voice was rising, like he no longer cared if people were looking.

"I'm afraid not," said the man. "You still need to be able to pay for the purchases. Go home and get a parent to check, or bring a card. We can keep your groceries here till you come back." He wasn't speaking unkindly but it was clear that there was no room for argument.

"Nooo!" Joe dropped his head down and his clenched fists were on the edge of the counter. Ice could tell that he was gritting his teeth and he was refusing to budge. Coming to her senses, she stepped quickly to his side by the counter.

"It's OK," she said. "Let him have the groceries. I can get these."

***

Joe made little puffing sounds as they walked and he kept his eyes fixed firmly on the pavement ahead of him. He hadn't thanked Ice, nor said a word to her since he had grabbed his groceries and stomped out of the shop. She didn't care. She didn't need to be thanked, but she wondered if she was supposed to try and calm him down or talk to him. He seemed furiously angry, but he had made no attempt to shake off her company, so she assumed that he wasn't cross with *her*.

"Glitches happen all the time, Joe," she tried, eventually. "Don't worry about it. Anyway, you got your stuff and that's good isn't it?"

"It's not a glitch!" His voice was angry and louder than before, but he kept his head down and did not look at Ice. "This is not about the technology and it's not my fault. It's *hers*, the stupid bag! It's a load of crap! What the hell am I supposed to do?"

This angry, rude Joe was not one that Ice had previously seen. He'd been inconsiderate and careless and this had sometimes made him act like a bully but it had always been accompanied by an air of humorous bravado which Ice recognised as essentially dishonest. It wasn't difficult to see that he wore it like a mask, though what he was trying to cover she was less sure about. He had never been overtly aggressive with her and she didn't like it. She was just about to part

61

company with him when he spoke again, this time with an obvious effort to be more measured.

"Look, sorry! I'm sorry. I didn't mean to go off on you and I'll pay you back. Cheers for getting me out of that. I was just, you know, embarrassed and stuff..." He tried to smile at Ice but it was not very successful and he sighed and dropped his gaze back to his feet. For a short while she walked beside him without answering. She fiddled with her hair, rehearsing what to say next.

"That's OK," she said, at last. "There's no hurry to pay me back or anything. Are you alright, though? You've got enough and all that? Is your mum OK?" Ice had never met Joe's mum. She wasn't at home on the couple of rare occasions when Ice had called round and otherwise Joe was generally out and about in the local neighbourhood on his own or with a couple of his horrible mates from school.

"Yeah, I'm fine. We're fine. I mean I hate all this and I wish we could just go back to how it was." He lifted up his bag of groceries by the handle, as if it was an emblem of the drought and the food shortages. "But I know everyone has to put up with it. Not just me! It's a real pain, but I'm fine. I'm the same as everyone else."

Ice nodded and continued beside him up the road in the direction of home. He was lying, of course. She knew that.

Chapter 11 ~ Fire

There were more fires that evening. The rise and fall of the sirens could be heard, intermittently, in the distance and closer on the main road at the bottom of the hill. Ice and Buddy peered out of the lounge window. She was checking which way the smoke was being blown and Buddy was looking to see what *she* was looking at. Buildings obscured the view, but over the tops of these she saw the characteristic bulging cones of grey which billowed upwards and then spread out, mingling together to turn the sky a dirty yellow-grey hue. Although they were too far away to be alarming, Ice felt for the people who lived in those areas and hoped the fire fighters would manage to get control and keep the flames away from the houses. They tended to break out first in the dry scrub and parched woodlands, but she knew homes could easily be ignited and took note of the direction of the smoke — thankfully away from this part of Depton.

She was still staring out when Oscar arrived on his bike, accompanied by Mr Cooper who had ridden to fetch him from his friend's house on the other side of town. Even if Buddy hadn't started barking as they came through the door, Ice would have picked up on the air of excitement.

"Oh my God that was so scary! Look, my hands are still shaking." Oscar was laughing breathlessly and holding up his hands for Ice, or Buddy or their dad to witness the evidence. They both had flushed faces, grimy with mingled sweat and ashy streaks. Her brother was lifting his T-shirt to rub his nose and eyes, making it worse. Droplets of blood were congealing where his bare arms and torso were scratched.

"What was? What happened?" Ice asked. Oscar was a fan of the dramatic, but the expression on her father's face was a good indicator that something had frightened them both.

"It's OK, we're fine," Mr Cooper replied, taking in a deep breath and blowing it out in a long stream. "We were a bit close to the fire, that's all. It could have been dangerous for a minute there, but we got out. Everyone's safe. We left the fire department to do their job. Well done, Oscar! Good cycling and following instructions."

Her dad's version played it down somewhat, as he always tended to do. Oscar's account was more disturbing. Although they were both unharmed, from what Ice heard, they had been at real risk of being trapped.

"It was amazing, Ice! You've no idea how fast a fire can travel till you're up close like that. I mean Dad and I were just riding on the cycle path that goes along Victoria Road and we could see the fires, like a way away – not very near. Probably that bit of land by the river. That floodplain where we sometimes walk the Bud. The smoke was going high up into the air but the fire engines came past us on the road. I had to put my finger in my ear – they were so loud!"

"Yes, I heard them, too," Ice interjected. "And you can see the smoke from here." She pointed to the window where the plumes were still rising visibly above the houses. "What happened? Why did you nearly get trapped? You didn't go towards the fires, did you?"

"No," Ice's father said. He lifted Oscar's left arm, examining the worst of the scratches. "Not too bad. Get those cleaned up, Oscar. Don't forget your face. Ice, would you mind giving him a hand?" This was her dad's way. He avoided making a fuss in front of them. It was a kind of protection.

Showing too much concern could be disturbing for young children. If the parents were scared, then there must be something to be scared of. It was better for Oscar, but Ice was in no doubt that her dad had been frightened too.

"I'll leave you to give the story to Ice if you like," he continued. "I'm just going clean up and then call Mum to let her know we're safe. She might be worried, knowing that we were out that way. You can use the kitchen sink, Oscar. Give yourself a wash and change your shirt."

Ice turned back to Oscar, who was rubbing Buddy's chest and inviting him to join a game of tug-of-war with a toy made from a couple of old socks. The adrenaline rush from the narrow escape had given him a burst of energy that felt like it needed dispelling somehow. Ice had to persuade him away so that he could clean his arms and face and relate what had happened without all the giggling and play growling. She had managed to settle him with a cup of tea and some toast at the kitchen table before he took up the story again.

"Of course we didn't cycle towards the fire, Ice. We're not that stupid! But it's weird when you're there. Like you always watch these things on video and think why don't people just get out of it or go the other way and stuff. But when it's real, it can get really confusing. One minute we were looking at the fire engines driving down the road and checking out the smoke, and then the next minute, it was all over the cycle path. It was really scary. Don't they say that most people die from the smoke and not the fire? Dad shouted to me to not breathe it in and to cover my nose and mouth with my T-shirt. That's really hard to do when you're riding! We were coughing and I could hardly see. The lights are all orangey inside a smoke cloud, like the sun is blotted out. Plus it's really hot and the bits of ash sting like hell. My eyes were streaming. Then dad grabbed my bike and kind of pulled me along. I thought we were both going to die."

"Wow!" Ice said. It was an inadequate response, but she was showing Oscar that she was paying attention and prompting him to continue. "So then what?"

"It was just luck, you know. We could've breathed in loads of that smoke and gone unconscious and died. We were lucky that the fire from the one side sort of sucked the air and made a kind of wind that cleared the path so we could see. Except there was another fire really close by. The tree by the path in front of us went up suddenly, like 'whoosh!'." He accompanied this with an upward fling of his hands to illustrate speed and direction, and looked up as if seeing the huge tower of fire in front of him. "Those flames were enormous. Bigger than anything I've ever seen at Bonfire Night. And they roar. Did you know that, Ice? Fire is really noisy!"

Ice gave Oscar a shocked look and shook her head, but didn't interrupt.

"So then we were there with this huge fire just in front and we were going to have to turn round and go back, but behind us it was all thick smoke again. Dad swore, Ice. He was using the 's' word loads – and worse ones!"

"What did you do?"

"We had to go over the hedge into a school field. We couldn't get to the gate, and I think it was locked anyway. Other people were running up the path. Dad picked up the bikes and kind of threw them both over. Then he lifted me up and dropped me on the other side of the fence in front of the hedge, and pushed me between a gap in the branches. I don't know how he got through himself. He's lucky he's not fat, is all I can say! We pedalled so quick then, over the field. I've never gone that fast cross country. I felt like the fire was chasing me!"

Oscar was breathing quickly again and now that the first flush of excitement and adrenaline was over, there was a catch in his voice and the slight wobble at the corners of his mouth that gave away just how afraid he had been. His eyes were still streaming with the effects of the smoke and he was fighting back real tears. Ice wanted to give him a cuddle, but she knew that would make him cry properly and embarrass him, so she said, rather more loudly and cheerily than she expected, "Well thank goodness you're both OK! One to tell the grandchildren when you're an old man with no teeth or hair left." She ruffled his scruffy locks as if to emphasise that he should make the most of them while he still had them. They were tacky with cinders and sweat and no longer visibly ginger. Ice rubbed her hands on her jeans. "Ew! You should probably give this a wash. Water's been on for a while."

Oscar nodded and swallowed his tea before moving over to the kitchen sink and pulling off his grimy T-shirt. He let Ice help him sponge down his arms with warm soapy water and then he splashed his face and dunked his head forward into the sink while Ice scooped cupfuls and poured it over for him. When the water was quite grey and his hair nearly back to its original colour again, she grabbed a clean tea towel and let him finish off drying himself.

"That's better," she said. "Go get a new shirt now and chuck that one in the laundry."

After Oscar had gone upstairs, Ice sat down again on one of the kitchen stools. They'd had a near miss. She should feel relieved that they were unharmed, and she did, but she wondered how safe they all were. She slid from her seat and returned to the front window to reassure herself that the fires had been dealt with and were not coming closer. The plumes still rose in the distance, and there was nothing nearby, but Ice stared, willing them to die down so that she could relax.

The smoke reminded her of pictures she'd seen of the clouds formed by bombs after they had been dropped, or of the vapours rising from erupting volcanoes. She knew it was just the burnt particles and ash, driven upwards by the heat, but they bulged and surged, making surreal shapes against the darkening sky as though they were living things from a science fiction film. It was natural to be scared of fire. All animals were. She tried not to think of those that were unable to escape. She hoped most of them would have found a place to run to.

She thought of the conversation she had had with Daniel. There had been huge forest fires in other parts of the world – Australia, Brazil, the USA. Footage of them on the news had shown people trying desperately to rescue creatures that had been burned or giving them water out of their drinking bottles. Sometimes they showed the blackened corpses of those that hadn't been so lucky. England didn't have koalas, but there were still native animals that had survived the drought. Who was going to rescue them? As if to confirm this thought, a flock of birds flew up from one of the chestnut trees, its top just visible above the houses this side of the smoke plumes. Then, as Ice watched, they circled and danced in the sky, spreading out from each other and converging again until they were no longer separate entities but formed the shape of a great beast – a stag, head held high, giant antlers raised, black against the reddish-brown backdrop of the smoky sky.

Ice ran. Her phone was still on the kitchen table. She needed to get evidence this time! She grabbed it and flicked it to video mode almost dropping it in her haste. She threw herself on to the couch by the front window and touched the red 'record' dot, pressing the phone against the glass, but the birds had already begun to disperse. When Ice replayed her video, she could still see where the shape of the stag was, if she looked carefully and knew what it had been, but to anyone else it would just be a flock of birds and one of those interesting but easily explained natural coincidences.

Chapter 12 ~ Marianne

Her parents had said things to reassure her, but Ice had stared at the smoke for a long time before she was confident enough to go to bed. When she did get to sleep, it was fitful and full of dreams of smoke enveloping the house and flames roaring up against her bedroom window. A couple of times she had to get up to check outside. Even then, when she had convinced herself that the fires were nowhere near, she could feel her heart pounding as though the danger were real. She was glad when daylight came so that she could give up the fight. Apart from seeing to Buddy, Ice put aside her personal calendar that morning and left the house early on her bicycle. She was relieved to see that the nearby fires had been apparently quenched since the previous night and that any columns of smoke were distant.

She had packed water, a roll of kitchen towel and had bungee-strapped a sturdy wooden box to her carrier. She had also typed a quick text and sent it to her parents and to Oscar, letting them know that she had gone out, promising it was only for a ride and that she would be careful and home by lunchtime.

The streets were quiet before the build up of work traffic. Though there was the faint tang of scorched vegetation on the air, it was cool from the night. Big things were weighing on everyone's mind but there were immediate, simple pleasures to appreciate still, like the sensation of the wind in your face and the freedom to ride fast without interruption.

Ice passed through now-familiar neighbourhoods where everything looked normal. Curtains were not yet drawn open and cars were parked in the driveway. Perhaps future historians would be able to look back at photographs of this period and see the evidence of a time of change: few cars were newer than ten years old and some of them were showing signs of not having moved for a while – tyres were a little flat, windows a little dirty.

The part of Depton Ice was heading for, was a flood meadow that true to its name, had been completely under water in the spring the year before. This was where the fires had been, according to Oscar in his breathless account the night before. It was a broad, flat area of ground that ran along the riverside and stretched out into a kind of scrubby meadow. Once the water had subsided last year, it had been an amazing place to visit because all manner of native plants had sprung up in the recently inundated soil. With them there had been a sudden boom in insects and other life. A lone feral peach tree grew there and had managed to survive the floods. As Ice arrived at the edge of the field, this was still its tallest feature, roughly in the middle, possibly from a peach stone dropped by a long gone picnic party. After all its years of surviving floods and droughts and the over-enthusiastic mowing of successive councils, it was deeply sad to see it now, no more than a blackened skeleton.

With a heavy heart Ice gazed at the scene. Leaving her bike propped against a concrete block that had been dumped at the edge to deter motorcyclists, she picked her way across the open area. The ground was charred and the prickly remnants of the grass crumbled to ash where she walked. Surprisingly, the burning had been patchy and she could see a clear definition where the fire had blackened a swathe of vegetation and then apparently been moved in another direction or perhaps been extinguished before it could go further. Some clumps of grass were still sticking up, pale brown and dry but unburned. Ice knew that the grass and other meadow plants would emerge green in the future, given half a chance and a little rain. Fire was part of their natural cycle and they had evolved to regrow or sprout from undamaged seeds afterwards. However, the floodplain was a thriving ecosystem and she thought sadly of the individual animals that would have suffered. She looked, hoping not to find casualties. Invertebrates like spiders and insects would probably have been vaporised by the heat, but the area was riddled with the burrows of small mammals and once, last summer, she had seen a grass snake make its rapid retreat towards the river.

If she did find something, she wasn't sure what she intended to do. She tried to imagine herself carrying out some sort of rescue operation. What would that entail? Maybe there'd be small mammals – hedgehogs, perhaps. Would she pick one up? And take it where? Half crouched, she bent down to see the ground and examine it more closely. Ice moved across the devastated terrain, but she found nothing – no animals, dead or half alive – and she was relieved.

"You won't find anything." This was a woman's voice that Ice vaguely recognised. Whilst she had been stooped, hands on knees studying the ground, she had not noticed that someone had approached. She was not pleased to see that it was the weird woman she and Joe had met at the Twelve Brothers.

"OK…" Ice replied quietly, standing up and beginning to move away. She was in no mood to deal with this woman's tales of doom this morning.

"Those that could leave, have gone and those that could not have been burned beyond trace," she went on. "You've seen it, haven't you? The great beasts are a warning to all who can understand. Do *you* understand? They are showing you."

Ice shook her head.

"I don't know what you're talking about. I'm just looking." Ice's reserve kept her from saying, "Please go away and leave me alone." though this is what she was repeating in her head as the woman made every sign that she was going to continue to talk at her, and when Ice walked towards the concrete slab where she had left her bike, the woman followed. Ice was taking hold of the handlebars when the woman called out, "Wait! I'm sorry – I don't mean to frighten you. I'm not mad."

"That's what mad people say," thought Ice, but it was enough to make her pause. The witch woman didn't look like she could be an actual threat, even with the feeling of discomfort Ice experienced. Her clothes and her demeanour were odd, that was true, but perhaps Ice was in no position to be judgemental about strangeness.

"Who are you and what do you want?" she asked.

"I'm Marianne. Sit," the woman replied, positioning herself on the concrete block and patting the space beside her. Ice did not obey and Marianne shrugged and continued anyway while Ice stood, holding her bicycle by the handles but not climbing on to the saddle.

"I know you've seen things," she went on. "I could tell when I first met you. You had the look of someone who has the gift."

Internally, Ice scoffed at this and visibly rolled her eyes. It was such a cliché!

"Oh yes, OK, I know, I know," Marianne said, "Ridiculous, yes? Like a film. But I think I'm right. You've seen the Little Ones, haven't you? In the past. They revealed themselves to you and showed you the truth. And now the giant beasts. Which ones? The Bull? The Bear? It's not for nothing that you have seen them."

It was unsettling to have someone – a complete stranger – talk about Ice's experiences like this as though she had intimate information. This woman didn't know her! How could she speak about the shadelings – and the bird creatures? The sensible part of Ice's nature was telling her to leave but something else compelled her to stay – that gratification of being able to share with another human being who understood. It was very seductive and she replied before she could stop the words from being spoken.

"A stag. And a horse." Instantly, she regretted letting the woman know that she was right. It was like giving her permission to go on.

"Ah yes, yes." Marianne responded, nodding. "Yes, I have seen those, too. And others. It's a bad sign. We need to prepare. And you need to heed them."

This was what Ice had wanted to avoid. It was hard enough dealing with the day-to-day situation without the ill omens. Besides, these were often not quite what people had imagined in their mythologies. The shadelings had been thought to be harbingers of doom from Hell and had turned out to be nothing of the sort. But Ice also knew that the woman was telling the truth – at least the truth as she saw it – and her curiosity won out.

"What are they and what do they mean? Prepare for what? What's going to happen? What am I supposed to do?" she asked. She placed the bike back against the block and half sat, half leaned against the concrete edge, next to Marianne, but not too close. Maybe this woman was a mad witch-lady but she seemed to know things. Things that Ice wanted to find out about.

"They have lots of names," Marianne replied. "Once they were named 'Bioccan'. Some know them as the 'Great Beasts'. I call them the 'Old Ones.' They have been here since before humans inhabited these islands. They can appear as mist, or swarms of insects… or flocks of birds…" she glanced at Ice, "…you have seen these, I think, but they are not real birds, nor are they real beasts. The Ancients thought of them as the spirits of the animals they knew. There are spirits in everything – the water, the trees, the rocks. This is the way we understand the forces of nature. Call them what you will. They exist. At this time of year, they are more readily seen, as the fabric between our worlds grows thin. Halloween is not just a chance for selling cheap man-made rubbish to consumers. It's Samhain – it's real. Those like myself, who follow the old religion can feel it. Those like you, who notice things, can notice it."

"I read about that," Ice interrupted, ignoring the last remark. "Also the spirits of our ancestors are supposed to come back and we can put food out and talk to them and stuff…"

Marianne looked at her and laughed. It annoyed Ice.

"Indeed," she replied. "So they say. Though I have never spoken to mine, nor shared so much as a sandwich! I have only seen the Old Ones, as you have. But never like this. In the past, I thought I was lucky to catch a glimpse once every few years. Even just a hint of a great beast in the pattern of the low-lying clouds. This is different, though, and I think you sense it, too. You have already seen them two, maybe three times. And not just a vague image that may be your imagination, but something clear and defined that you cannot doubt."

Ice nodded, slowly. It was true – and now she wished that it weren't, because it gave credence to the other part of Marianne's story. That something dreadful was going to happen and that they needed to 'prepare'.

Chapter 13 ~ Panther

Ice left her strange companion without feeling the need for a polite parting ritual. Perhaps it was the way the woman had imposed her company twice now, without introductions that meant she could skip the formalities, because when there was a momentary pause, Ice simply got up, said, "I'm going now." and cycled off.

She was aware, as she pedalled, that this was the route Oscar and her dad must have taken. She thought she might have spotted the charcoal trunk and remaining branches of the tree that had burst into flame in front of them, but she was sad to see that there were several possible candidates. On this side of the road, none of the trees had been spared and the smell of burnt wood was still strong in the air. Opposite, was the fence and the hedge that ran along the school field. She could visualise her father lifting the bikes above his head and throwing them on the other side, before helping his son to safety and clambering over, himself.

Though the sun had begun to make its mark, the morning was still fresh, and cooler than it would be later on in the day so instead of heading home, Ice rode on until she was past the blackened devastation. The dedicated cycle path took her half a mile or so along the main route used by the schoolchildren from that part of Depton, and then it ended suddenly. Cyclists who intended going further were forced on to the road or to share a narrow pavement with pedestrians. It was typically ridiculous, Ice thought and she half contemplated returning home, but did not. Without the school traffic, there was a peaceful stillness and solitude that she was not ready to give up just yet.

Although the lorry incident was in the back of her mind, Ice took the less safe but also less annoying option of riding on the road. This meant not having to stop at every minor junction and she could freewheel at speed down the hills. Besides, there were no cars at all, even at the main roundabout on the edge of town. She slowed down sufficiently to see that the way was clear to her right and then crossed straight over, taking the road that led her away from the last of the buildings and into the countryside.

On either side of the route were fields that held a late wheat crop which the farmer had yet to harvest. She felt sure it was overdue – by now, they should be sowing for the following autumn. She wondered if the farmer would bother. Somehow the plants had coped with the lack of rain for this season – irrigation, probably – but they wouldn't manage if the drought didn't break next year. Despite their uncertain future, the fields, were a glorious sight – an expanse of gold in the intense light.

Gradually, the open space gave way to a lane more densely edged by autumnal trees, and bushes covered in ivy which was still stubbornly green in spite of everything. Ice gained speed on a downward stretch and gave up the pedalling, letting gravity do the work. The momentum carried her halfway up the next rise before she had to push again to reach the crest of the hill, enclosed in a small wood. Here, she paused for a minute to catch her breath and to listen for bird sounds. It was ominously quiet. On the air she caught the unmistakable scent of something dead.

She knew that smell. Last year, she and Buddy had come across the corpse of a fox that had been left by the subsiding flood water and had lain rotting in the sun, its skull already half exposed by maggots. Now, moving on to the downside of the hill, Ice saw the source. A badger had met its fate as a victim of roadkill. She felt for it, poor thing. The black and white fur was matted with congealed blood but its head had been crushed by the tyre of some long gone hit-and-run and Ice consoled herself with the knowledge that it would have been an instant death. It was a better way to go than being caught in a fire, or to die slowly in a trap.

She waited, seated on the saddle, brakes gripped to hold the bike steady, one foot on the ground. A glossy, black crow was making a meal of the grisly remains in the middle of the road. It caught her eye and for a few seconds the two of them stared at each other, neither moving. Then it continued, obviously deciding Ice was not worth further interruption. She wished it well. Crows were brilliant birds – highly intelligent and with a knack for survival. Although it was a gruesome scene, Ice found herself smiling and reaching for her phone to snap the picture.

Suddenly the crow bounced into the air and flapped off, just above Ice's head and into the wood. She caught her breath. It had been frightened by the approach of something bigger – something familiar to Ice. This time there was no mistaking the large feline creature that stood not more than three metres away. It was definitely no mythical beast which might dissolve into a flock of birds. This was a real panther, almost black, but with the recognisable markings of a leopard visible in its dusky coat. It glared at her – yellow irises a vivid contrast to the dark fur – and snarled. Ice's heart hammered in her chest but she remained rooted to the spot by a mixture of fear and fascination. As quietly and with as little movement as possible, she pressed the capture button on her phone.

wincing as it emulated the shutter sound of a camera. The animal was not interested in her, though, because it bent down, shoulders hunched, and gripped the badger carcass with two sets of huge incisors, lifting the whole thing off the tarmac. She remained transfixed as it hauled away its prize, padding silently on enormous paws down the quiet Warwickshire lane before turning into a side road. When Ice was brave enough, she followed, pedalling to the junction, but she could not see it. The destinations at the crossroads were marked with the small, white signs of the English countryside. Depton was labelled as the way she had come, but of the other three, one name stood out. She had heard it recently and she had seen it written. With a flash of interest, Ice read the sign pointing up a narrow lane flanked by dusty conifers and russet ash trees that broke up the mid-morning light. It was the road to Bale.

Chapter 14 ~ Bale

Bale. It was a creepy-sounding place and Ice felt a chill in spite of the sun that was nearing noon. She glanced at her phone and cursed inwardly for having said she'd be back by lunchtime, because she would never make it now. It was good to feel free, but it was never quite true. Having people who worried about you was always a bit of a shackle. You had to tell them where you were going and let them know when you'd be back. She sent a text to her father to say that she was on a ride and would see him in a few hours. Ice contemplated the lane that wound into the distance, three and a half miles to Bale, according to the sign. She had already ridden six from Depton, she noticed, and was in two minds about whether to go back or to explore further. She opted for the second choice. If she went a little way on, she might spot the panther again.

It was a typical English winding country lane, cut between two banks without much of a verge. Along the route, the vegetation changed from woodland to prickly hedgerows. These were mostly bare of all but the driest leaves, though they sported clusters of small, red berries and other fruits that looked like tiny, dark plums. The branches made a dense barrier that was taller than Ice, even when she stood on the bike pedals. As a cyclist, there was nowhere for her to get out of the way of any vehicles that might try to pass, and she wondered how the panther normally fared. It had an uncanny ability to emerge suddenly and disappear back into seeming impenetrable undergrowth. She pedalled slowly, primed to detect any movement that might be the animal she sought. She knew it was risky behaviour. The large cat hadn't been that bothered by her, but it was a predator nonetheless. If it felt threatened, it might attack, but her desire to see it again was greater than her sense of danger.

Ice smelled the animals before she saw them. It was the odour of living creatures kept together in enclosures – the mixture of faeces and warm fur. She had come a mile down the road to Bale when the smell made her pull up next to a gate that closed off a dirt road leading up a slight rise to a farmhouse. At the fence, stood a single scruffy brown pony with a larger companion standing a little way off in the paddock. The pony whickered and looked at Ice sorrowfully out of one eye. The other was hidden beneath its long, tangled forelock of hair.

"Hello," she said. She dismounted, leaned the bike against the gate and reached over to stroke the creature's soft muzzle. The pony mumbled the palm of Ice's hand briefly before flicking its head up in frustration that she wasn't offering it anything tasty.

"I'm sorry. I haven't got something for you," Ice went on. She looked about but the drought had dessicated all the long grass. The ponies had scoured their field bare and now had only the bales of hay and straw that had obviously been strung up for them. Ice reached over and patted the creature firmly on the neck. It had a musky, comforting odour but this was not the same smell that had made Ice stop. Looking up to the buildings by the field, she could just make out a collection of structures built slightly away from the main house. The sounds of animals drifted down to her, strange and incongruous in the English farmyard setting. Ice lifted the gate latch and closing it behind her, rode up the dirt road towards the source.

By the time she arrived at the cages, she was no longer surprised at what she found. It was obvious. The panther, the smells, the strange calls. The owner of this property had a taste for exotic pets. Somehow they had managed to get hold of several different species, not all of which were familiar to Ice, but she recognised two of them as lemurs. At Ice's approach, they came to the chicken-wire stapled to the front of their wooden enclosure. In a disconcertingly human-like manner, they both clasped the metal with their front paws and pushed their little black and white snouts through the gaps between the wires. She felt a swell of emotion for the small prisoners. It was all she could do to stop herself breaking them free right there.

In the next cage was some kind of wild cat that pressed itself up against the far wall and hissed at her. Three birds were cooped together, competing for space on a couple of branches that had been placed there as perches. These were bright blue parrot-like birds – macaws, she thought – and clearly the source of the exotic sounds she had heard from the road. In the last, huddled together, were a group of five small, sandy foxes with enormous ears. All had their heads turned in Ice's direction, fixing her with a wary gaze. Her heart dropped at the sight of the inhabitants. Although they looked well cared-for and each cage was clean, with food and water visible, they were all a long way from home and confined in spaces that were impossibly small compared with what would have been their natural range.

Beside this row of wooden cages was a larger enclosure fenced with the same chicken-wire, and empty, apart from a couple of large logs and a dry water trough. Around the perimeter, next to the fence was a path that had been worn into the dusty soil by the repeated pacing of its former occupants.

Ice glanced over at the house, aware that she was trespassing. Then she took her phone from her backpack and filmed the animals in their cages. She wished she knew what to do for the poor creatures. The RSPCA used to prosecute people – but that was for obvious cruelty or neglect. Perhaps the owners were breaking the law by keeping them. Was anyone still checking things like illegal smuggling of exotic pets? Would that make any difference? People seemed to get away with things like that. And did she really want to alert authorities who might come out with a gun to shoot the escaped panther on the grounds of 'public safety'? Ice glanced back up to the farmhouse and was unnerved to see that someone was taking strides towards her. She was not prepared for a confrontation. Holding the handlebars clumsily with her phone still in one hand, she pushed on the pedal and rode furiously towards the gate, leaping off on arrival, just long enough to open it and get through, before cycling full speed away from the farm and up the lane towards Bale. She could hear one of the ponies whinnying as she fled.

Ice eventually stopped when she felt sure that she had put sufficient distance between herself and the owner of the private zoo. She was out of breath and panting from the exertion and the close call. What might the person have done, anyway? She was glad to not have to find out.

The road here had opened out slightly with a wider grassy verge. She had stopped next to another gate to her left. It looked very ordinary – like a farm gate – tubes of steel, welded together. Two strips of rough tarmac led away towards an area hidden by larger evergreens. A metre or so back from

the gate and running the length of the road as far as she could
see in either direction, was a green metal fence, topped with
rolls of razor wire. Behind this grew tall trees that would
normally have obscured the view of the grounds. Next to the
gate, secured to the fence and facing the road, was a large,
white sign which read:

MINISTRY OF DEFENCE
NO ADMISSION WITHOUT PERMISSION

Beside this, on two wooden poles stuck into the ground,
was a smaller one with the same black-on-white upper case
writing which warned trespassers to keep out and that they
were liable to 'arrest, removal, prosecution and fine under the
explosives act of 1975'.

She rode a little way further to where the trees became
more sparse. From here she could see through to some squat
red brick buildings dotted among some raised mounds, and
some roads that led to a flat parking area for vehicles. With
sudden recognition, she saw that there were half a dozen of
the tanker lorries, like the ones that had passed on their way
back from the common. Like the one that had rolled itself
into a ditch the day they had seen the Beast of Bale for the
first time.

***

She made it home by 2pm – early enough for there to be no
questions about where she had been. "Nice ride?" was all her
father had said to her and Ice had nodded without
explanation. Maybe later. She did have some evidence on her
mobile, after all. Seated at her computer, Ice scrolled through

her phone album. The shots were still there, she was relieved to see. For now, at least. The deletion of film of the accident from all their phones had spooked her, and she could feel her heart-rate rising, even at the thought that she might have opened herself up to investigation by some 'authority' or worse. You heard stories of what happened to 'whistle blowers' or people who became too much of a nuisance for big companies. She was still worried about Mia, though she hadn't spoken to her, nor Daniel, since the incident. Nevertheless, she wanted to keep the photographs. She backed them up as well as she could, using an old USB cable to save them to the hard drive of her mum's ancient PC. Ice wasn't sure whether that was safe. She supposed hackers could look at anybody's computer as long as it was connected to the net, but it felt more secure that way than on her phone where who knows who could see your apps.

Ice indulged in a moment of self-congratulation. The photographs on the large screen were stunning. She had captured the crow in mid flight, wings beating the air, legs out to one side as it prepared to fly past her. It was a great shot, in spite of, or maybe because of, the blurred parts showing movement. The following picture was better still. It could have been a scene from the tropics – the panther was stooping to lift its prey, head down, teeth visible. Ice took a deep breath and sat back, admiring the view on the screen for several seconds.

She knew that there was a certain 'illicit' quality about the video shots that followed – those of the private zoo – and she felt that surge of sympathy again, having time to look at the faces of the captive animals staring out of the screen. She would show these to her parents later. Her mum would share

Ice's dismay and maybe she would know what could be done. However, those were not the shots that caused her pulse rate to rise. She looked at the photo of the signs again. They made it clear in no uncertain terms that what went on at that location was not something for the general public. Trespassers would be arrested! It wasn't a good idea to take on the military. Ice knew that people in other countries had found themselves in deep trouble by inadvertently taking snaps of places like this – and she had done it deliberately!

On the large screen in front of her, was a picture of the trees and the plot of land, with the car-park in the distance. The vehicles looked small from her vantage point, but she could see them. Whatever that lorry had been carrying that day when it had crashed, it was destined for this installation. She didn't delete the pictures from her phone, but thought better of including them with the images of the panther when she sent a message to Mia and Daniel.

> hi guys. how you both? shared some pics. look at this! it's real after all. saw it when out on bike today!

She added a shocked face and a cat emoji before continuing.

> sad thing, though. looks like it escaped from this place. someone keeping animals on their farm. panther seems OK, but those poor little guys. what do you think I should do?

"What are they?" It was Oscar asking. Ice hadn't realised he was in the house. He hovered in the doorway and Ice wondered if it was because he was respecting her privacy. Buddy had no such qualms, though, pushing past Oscar and giving Ice his stump-tailed wag while she tried to protect her phone from his exuberance and his spittle.

"Oi! Sit!" she commanded, before waving Oscar in. She looked at the picture that was still displayed on the computer.

"I think they're fennec foxes. I found a sort of private zoo thing on a farm while I was out riding. They had them caged outside. Look there are others." She flicked through the pictures, showing Oscar and describing how she had not stayed around to face the owner.

"I lost my nerve, but now I feel guilty because I think I should have done something," she said.

"Aw, the lemurs are really cute," Oscar replied. "It's like they've got little hands, the way they're holding on." He indicated to Ice to move to one side so that he could join her on the chair. She shifted over a little, letting him sit down. Not many people could invade her space like that without her having to leave. Her little brother was one of the very few. She had been five years old when he was born and she vaguely remembered her parents trying to make sure that she did not feel left out or usurped by the new baby. They needn't have worried. She had paid him almost no attention at all. It was like he was just another object they had purchased for the house. A new lamp or a piece of furniture. He not made any difference to her and she was no more jealous of the attention he got than if he had been a pot plant that had needed watering.

Without her realising it, Oscar had won over the young Ice. He had a baby's lack of respect for boundaries and somehow she had accepted this in the way that she did with other animals. Most people warmed quickly to the cheerful good nature of this little boy, but it had been Ice who had been there for him later when he had needed it – when their mother had been away for increasing periods of time and when Oscar had woken distressed and the sheets had been wet. In his turn, Oscar had never made Ice feel odd. Whatever she told him, no matter how bizarre, he always managed to accept it as the sort of thing that *could* happen.

"Yes, I know. They were sweet," she answered him, "But it's not really OK, is it? Keeping wild animals – and not even from here – in cages on a farm. I don't think that can be legal. I'll ask Mum later. There must be something we can do. Those animals weren't happy in there. How could they be? Stuck in those little boxes all their lives."

"Yeah – you're right," Oscar said. "People are weird. If you like animals, why would you want to make them prisoners?"

Ice shrugged.

"Funny you should say that, though. Not all of them are still captive. Here's one that got away!"

Oscar made the silent 'o' shape with his mouth that he always did when he was amazed or impressed. Ice smiled at his admiration. The panther was pretty spectacular.

"You took that today?"

She wasn't sure if it was a statement or a question, but she nodded.

"It's not the first time, actually. I saw it last Friday with Daniel and Mia. The day that lorry crashed and Mum was home late. Only we were too slow to get a picture on our phones. That's almost certainly what it was." She pointed at the photograph displayed on the screen. "It must have quite a range, because this is miles from where we saw it last time."

"It is *so* cool!" Oscar said. "Do you have any more?"

"Not really. Only these. There's a sort of military base by Bale. It looks all bit top secret – or dangerous, perhaps. They don't want anyone in there, at any rate. These signs are on the fence and look, it's razor wire so people don't climb over."

"It looks well sinister," her little brother added. "I bet there are dodgy things there. Like maybe nuclear bombs. Or – I know – they've probably got UFO bits that they're keeping secret. Like alien technology and stuff. They will be using it to build special weapons or something that can fly really fast or be invisible. It's the kind of thing they do in those places."

Ice laughed despite the feeling she shared with Oscar that the place had a chilling atmosphere to it. The truth was usually much more simple. It was more likely just a military place where they carried out manoeuvres and didn't want the public getting hurt.

"It says 'explosives', Oscar," she said. "They don't want people to get accidentally blown up!"

He wasn't deterred.

"Looks like they're keeping animals, too. Or maybe they're making genetically modified creatures, because that's really not right," her brother was saying.

"What do you mean?"

"What is that, do you think?" he said, pointing. He had his finger touching the screen on the left of the photograph with the parked trucks, showing some of the wooded area that screened out the majority of the buildings. Ice leaned in and peered. She zoomed in to the part Oscar was indicating. Yes. What was that?

"It looks like a bear. We don't still have bears in England, do we?" he asked. "So that's probably something they've engineered. A hideous mutant experiment." He seemed more pleased than surprised, as though it confirmed for him what he already knew about the dastardly goings on at the base.

Ice did not agree with him. She was getting used to seeing the giant creatures by now. She took it as a sign. There was more to see in Bale. There was more to do.

Chapter 15 ~ Shoes

Oscar was not the only one impressed by the picture of the panther. Mia's reply to Ice, was a string of emojis to show applause and astonishment. In her text, she wondered what Daniel's response had been, writing that she had not heard from him and maybe he was still feeling a bit rough from the flu. Ice agreed. He hadn't replied yet but she was sure he would like the picture. He might even want to take a trip with Ice – and Mia perhaps, though she wasn't much of a cyclist – to Bale to see if they could see it again. She would suggest it for when he was over his virus.

Ice surprised herself with the positive feeling that this thought gave her. She was looking forward to seeing her friend again – perhaps a little more than she expected. Daniel was good company, that was for sure, and she found that she was missing him. She liked how grounded and easy-going he was. The way he approached problems with a sensible attitude that made him look for solutions, even when they weren't always obvious. Daniel wore his heart on his sleeve. In that respect, he was the opposite to Ice, and it meant his company was never a strain. It would have been nice to talk to him right now.

Being on her own had never troubled her. It was not the same thing as being lonely. Solitude was just a physical state and if you liked your surroundings and the activity that you were doing, it was great. That was different to the mental state of feeling alone – that lack of human connection. The feeling that you had nobody 'on your side'. Ice counted herself lucky. Her family may have had their issues, but they were pretty good. Neither parent had been part of a conventional family unit growing up, but they'd done their best. True, her mother's work had meant long trips away, but the move here had been made in large part to put an end to those. And the friendships Ice had made right at the beginning in Depton had lasted and grown. She imagined showing Daniel the route to Bale, just the pair of them cycling up to the farm where the zoo was, and she realised how much she wanted to do this. Not just because it would be good to share it with someone, but because it would be good to share it with *him*.

Ice sent him a message.

> hey. how you doing? still not well? hope you feel better soon. did you like pic? wanna take ride up there when you recover from nasty bugs?

She followed this with a sickness emoji of someone looking green.

Ice contemplated her phone for a minute and when no message came back, she assumed Daniel was probably in bed, maybe trying to sleep off the virus, poor lad. Her room had gone quiet since Oscar and Buddy had returned to some other part of the house but she could hear her father banging stuff around. Every now and then there was the sound of a car door being shut. When she looked out of the window, she could see that her father had the boot open and was filling it up with bags of what looked like dog-food.

She was still wondering if she should contact the RSPCA about the private zoo, or wait until her mother returned for advice, when her father's voice cut through her thoughts and she jumped slightly at the sudden sound, not expecting him to be upstairs.

"These must belong to your friend." He was standing in the doorway to her room, holding out by the straps, a white cloth bag with a faded blue logo. Ice frowned, wondering which friend he was talking about and why her dad would have their bag of stuff. She reached for it as he brought it to her, and peered inside, staring at the scruffy trainers for several seconds before the penny dropped. Joe, again. These must be his shoes, left that day school closed and he had stayed for dinner. It was like some uncanny knack he had of cropping up uninvited in Ice's life. If it wasn't him personally, then it was his footwear! She let out a short groan and a huff of air, dropping her head in annoyance. If she'd had his phone number, she would have messaged him to come and fetch them – but she didn't have it.

"Yes – they're Joe's. I'll take them round," she said. "I'm walking Buddy in a minute. I'll do it then."

"Everything OK?" he asked.

"Yes – what are you doing, though? I could hear you moving things about downstairs. Are you having a clearout? Why are you loading the car?" The instant she spoke the words, she knew the answer, still hoping it would be something different. His response was typical Dad – evasive and not reassuring.

"I'm just packing some things. You know. In case. It's nothing to get worried about. I like to be prepared – that's all."

Ice closed her eyes and inhaled slowly. Then she simply said, "Dad..." in a tone that let him know she expected the truth.

He pulled at his top lip. It was a familiar gesture that he always seemed to make at times like this when he was figuring out whether to tell the whole truth or hold things back to protect the children. He knew that keeping things from Ice in the past had not been a good idea, but old habits died hard with Mr Cooper. He was a lot like her in that way. Her dad sighed and sat on Ice's bed.

"Alright," he said. "Remember we were talking about maybe having to leave if it got a bit too difficult here? Your mum and I agreed that we should make sure that the car was stocked up if we needed to go in a hurry. I have to confess, I was a bit spooked by the fire and even though they seem to have got them under control for now, it made me really remember all those news stories of people in Australia and the US having to evacuate their homes and flee with nothing. So… well… we have the opportunity to go away for a bit. Up North. It could almost be like a holiday… just for a while… um… till things, you know… if things settle down here a bit…"

She had known this was coming but still Ice felt a cold feeling in the pit of her stomach. What was this human tendency to believe that things would go on as they always had? It was a comforting deception to help people survive and make decisions and plans, and it was rubbish! Big changes could happen and did happen. Ice knew that this was one of those times. If they left Depton, it wouldn't be 'just for a while'. Things wouldn't 'settle down'. There would be no coming back.

"OK," she said, flatly. She felt sorry for her dad. What must it be like to have the responsibility of the whole family weighing on your mind? He probably hadn't thought about the danger and the stress and the scary future when he had decided he'd like to have children. Or did people really decide? Was it all just biology? Well… protecting your offspring was certainly biology and she understood why he was preparing to take them away from here to some place far away. A place with rain, perhaps. Without the threat of being engulfed in flames.

"Up North?" she asked. "Where? And when?"

"Well it's kind of a lucky thing, Ice, and something that tipped my hand, because there's a place where we can go. A cottage, in fact. In the North of Scotland not far from the coast. I had no idea about it. It belonged to your grandmother. Apparently she lived there with her second husband. My 'stepfather', I suppose. I didn't even know she'd died until the solicitor called me. It seems that I'm the sole heir."

Ice raised her eyebrows a little at this. She had never met her grandmother and she had never heard her dad refer to a stepfather before. It was one of those family stories that she vaguely knew but that they did not talk about much. Her dad had been raised by his father after his mother had left them. He had never expressed bitterness towards his absent parent. He always talked about his childhood as having been a happy one. Her grandad had done a good job of filling the gap, perhaps. Her dad's stories were of the times he and his father had built models together out of household items and about the museums and air shows they had visited. She remembered her grandad as a quiet, kind old man who made her buttered toast when they visited. He had died when she was nine and Ice vaguely recalled her father's grief as a confusing side to him that she was not used to. Now it looked like the mother who had abandoned her child could finally, posthumously even, be something of a parent and provide her son and the grandchildren she had never met with a safe place to go.

"We might need to leave soon, Ice, actually," he continued, cutting across her thoughts.

She nodded and said, "OK," again. There wasn't much else that could be said. It seemed like the conversation was now over because there was a pause which became an awkward moment and then her dad stood up and made to leave the room. He had been open with her. Perhaps she should do the same.

"Dad, there is something, actually. Maybe you can give me some advice."

He looked a little surprised and pleased.

"Of course," he said. "I'll try. What is it?"

Chapter 16 ~ Revelation

Ice mulled over her father's response, on the way to Joe's house. Buddy was keen to investigate the new smells and was pulling her to a stop at every pee spot along the way. She did not have the energy to insist that he walk nicely to heel, which anyway was always a bit of a hard task with the rescued boxer. His manners had improved, mostly thanks to the 'tellings off' he had received from other dogs in the encounters he'd had in the first months of his adoption, but he was still physically and mentally strong. Sometimes it was easier to just keep a bit of slack lead so that she didn't have her arm yanked at every post.

It gave her time to consider her dad's words. She scored them high for 'sensible' but not so much for 'helpful'. He had reinforced what she already knew. The animals were being 'well' looked after. The owners probably had a permit and if they didn't there was no longer an official body that was interested in that sort of thing. There was also nowhere for them to go that wouldn't involve another cage. The panther may have made its escape and be roaming free, but it should really be found and brought back and the others couldn't just be let out. They were very unlikely to survive and it was never a good idea to release 'exotics'. It might just be better to leave it alone and not interfere.

She had reluctantly come to this conclusion herself, by the time she reached Joe's front door. The 'authorities', whoever they might be, were mostly concerned with the humans in the area and had their hands full dealing with the drought and the fires. Animals were low down on the list of priorities – unless they posed a threat, in which case they'd surely just be killed as

the most convenient solution, under the pretence of 'safety'.
Her dad was probably right.

Buddy snuffled excitedly at the bottom of the door, eager
to explore this new territory and its inhabitants. Hanging in
the bay window to Ice's left, were heavy velvet curtains, a deep
red fading to pink at the edges from years of bleaching in the
sunlight. These were drawn so that they shielded the front
room from view. Some people were odd, she thought. It must
have been dark and gloomy inside, but maybe it was an
attempt to keep things cool in the way that the French did
with their wooden shutters – closed during the heat of the day.
She pressed the button for the doorbell and could hear an
echoing ring from the hallway inside. She wondered if Joe was
in. If not, she'd be relieved and could just leave the shoes on
the front step and escape without having to interact.

She stood examining the parched remnants of the plants
that grew in the tiny front plot. Once upon a time, somebody
had obviously tried to make it attractive, but it looked as
though it had been neglected long before the drought had hit.

Buddy gave a couple of short barks and she turned her
head, following the direction of his upturned muzzle. As she
did so, she registered an almost imperceptible shift in the
curtains. They had been parted so that a tiny slit was just
evident, as though someone wanted to peer out without being
noticed. Framed in this gap, just visible and on a level with
Ice's own, was a single dark eye. The owner and Ice stared at
each other for a few seconds, both conscious that they had
been seen but neither moving nor speaking, until Ice felt an
urge to burst out laughing. Finally she opened her hands in the
wordless, shrugging gesture of, "Well?" and the eye

disappeared into the gloom. A few seconds later, Joe pulled open the front door, keeping it just ajar.

"Yes? What?" he asked, peeping out but not opening it further.

She stretched her arm out towards him, the bag dangling by the straps.

"Oh," he said. "I didn't even know I'd left them at your house. It's not like I'm doing a lot of PE at the moment. But thanks."

He reached awkwardly through the gap in the door towards the bag and Ice handed it over without ceremony. He was being weird, but that wasn't unusual. Nevertheless, she was prompted to ask, "You OK?" and then to realise that he really was not, in spite of of his dismissive response. He looked guilty – furtive about something. She wouldn't put it past him to have done something illegal and to be on the look out. If that were the case, she really did not want to know.

"Right," she said, shrugging. "Well, bye, then." She turned to leave, her hand already on the small, metal gate that led into the front patch, but Buddy was resistant. He had other ideas, pulling her back and barging his way past Joe into the hallway so that she was forced to drop the lead or be dragged in after him.

"Buddy, no! Here!" she shouted, knowing that it would not make any difference. He had no sense of respect for the privacy of humans and after an enthusiastic sniff round Joe's knees, went on inside to explore further.

"I'm so sorry. He's a bit headstrong! Can you get him or do you need me to come in?"

Joe cracked a faint smile – a shadow of his former cheeky grin. He wiped the backs of his legs which were damp from

Buddy's nose and turned to look where the dog had run into the house, probably to sniff out the kitchen. At home, Buddy had free reign. When they had first brought him from the rescue centre, they had some crazy idea that he was to know his place and stay downstairs. It had only taken one night to give in, feeling guilty and sorry for him. He'd spent three years in bad homes and kennels. Keeping company with his new human 'pack' at night was the least they could do.

Joe leaned into the door-frame and dropped his head, shaking it like a gesture of defeat. Then he opened the door fully and waved Ice in.

It was a couple of degrees cooler inside Joe's house and it had a smell that reminded Ice of second-hand shops — a kind of mustiness mingled with the odour of humans. Joe was wearing just a vest and shorts and his feet were bare. His hair looked unwashed and tousled, like he had just woken up.

Ice followed him through the living room and into the kitchen, where Buddy had his muzzle down at the bottom of the back door and was making huffing noises at the smells coming in from outside. His world was awash with exciting olfactory information.

"Oi you!" Ice said, in a mock reprimand. She picked up the end of the lead which was trailing on the floor and then turned back to Joe. She had not failed to notice the state of the house.

"Joe, what the hell is going on?"

The kitchen was completely bare. A couple of the wall cupboards were open and Ice could see that they were empty. Cleared out. The living room, through which they had passed, had nothing in it apart from a single, battered sofa against one wall and the indentations in the carpet as evidence of the furniture which had previously stood there.

Joe looked defensive, but he said, rather too loudly, "Well you might as well know now! She's gone! The old bag. She's left. They've taken everything, more or less. Apart from that shitty old van of her boyfriend's which he left to rot away in one of those garages at the back. Not much use to me, is it? No tax, no MOT. Not even worth much as scrap. I suppose I could sell the fuel if there's any left."

Ice knew what had happened. She could picture it in her mind's eye. It was a knack she had of visualising past events which had taken place in a particular location. The image of Joe's mother was not very clear, but the rest of it was. The teenager returning late one afternoon, hungry as he always was these days, finding the door locked – no sign of his parent. The car gone from the street outside. Joe, not unused to being locked out, making his own way in through the open window at the back. His increasingly desperate journey through the whole house – all rooms gutted apart from his bedroom.

"You can't tell anyone!" He was speaking urgently. It was a half command, half plea.

"What? No, OK... I mean… Your mum has left? Without you?" It was silly to be asking, because she already knew the answer. She felt she needed to say something. To confirm the nasty truth.

"What does it look like?" he replied, looking down and stroking Buddy's ears and changing the subject without a pause, "Shall we let him out the back, then?"

He did not wait for Ice to answer before turning the key that was still in the lock and opening the door for Buddy to run out. Ice followed Joe into the small yard. It was not much more than a few metres in all directions, walled on all sides and mostly paved in grey concrete blocks. In the cracks had grown weeds – the first colonisers of abandoned urban settings – though they had also become dry and yellow. There was a strip of earth at one side and here the plants had fared better, some of them still looking robust and drought resistant, but all the evidence was that there had been little human intervention for a while. A variety of items were strewn about the yard and stacked up against the brick walls that enclosed it: plastic tubs that had become brittle and begun to shatter; the mangled skeleton of a rotary clothes line; an old car battery; some black rubbish bags that had been dumped by the back gate.

Joe dropped himself down on a wooden bench on the opposite side of the derelict flower bed and gazed up at Ice as though he was waiting for her to speak. She unclipped the lead from Buddy's collar and wrapped it into a coil around her hand, sitting next to Joe as she did so.

"What are you going to do?" she asked.

Joe shrugged.

"There's not a lot I can do," he said. "Stay here for now, while I can. But sooner or later, they're going to know that nobody is paying the rent and then I can't be here or they'll try and put me in some sort of 'care'. And that could be anything. Who's still fostering difficult teenagers these days? People who aren't doing it for any *good* reasons, that's for sure! I think I'd rather just take my chances out there." He gestured towards the back gate as though that would cover the concept of roaming homeless on his own.

Ice had no doubt that Joe was used to being alone 'out there', but she did not rate his chances of surviving in the long term. He was very likely to draw attention to himself through some misdemeanour or an act of careless bravado. Then he would end up in care anyway – or worse! The very first time Ice had met him, he had been making trouble. She wondered what would be going through his head. How does it feel to be abandoned by the person who is supposed to care for you? It made her think of her father. Their stories were so similar, but so different. Her father had always had one loving parent. Joe was less lucky.

"I won't tell anyone if you don't want me to, but maybe someone can help. Like... is your father... or... I mean, my parents might know what to do. Or, you know, Mrs King or something? She's on the Town Council. She knows you. Sort of."

Joe shook his head vehemently. He ignored the mention of his father.

"Ice, they're adults. They'll try to do the 'proper thing' won't they? That's bad news for me. Look, I'll be fine. I can take care of myself and I can stay here until I think of something. I'm glad she's gone. I'm free now. I can go anywhere and do anything. I don't have to put up with her rubbish any more! She's obviously decided she doesn't give a damn about me! And for goodness' sake don't get the blond bombshell involved! He's got enough to feel superior about without this!"

Ice was not good with euphemisms. She had to rack her brains for a minute to understand who Joe was referring to. Blond bombshell? What an odd term!

"What... Daniel? He's not superior! He doesn't act like he is. Anyway, he helped me out when I needed it and so did Mrs King. But whatever. Stay here alone if that's what you want."

She could hear the annoyance in her own voice. Why was that? Joe had a way of making her cross. She should leave him to his own devices if he did not want help. She rose to clip Buddy back on the lead.

"Right. I'd better get him walked properly," she said turning to face Joe. He was still seated on the bench, hands dropped between his knees, head down. Ice felt a jolt of shock, as though suddenly seeing him properly. He looked so young and pathetic and half-starved. The signs had been there but she had not really registered how vulnerable he was. Perhaps it was his cocky air, or the fact that he irritated her so much that had made her a bit indifferent to his suffering. He was still a child – a young sixteen – alone in a world that was growing increasingly hostile, with no resources and little chance. She could not really leave him to his own devices.

"Joe," she said, and he looked up at her. "I'll bring you some more food. Do you still have your phone?"

He nodded. "Still works for now. Contract runs out at the end of next month. She won't renew it."

"Let me have your number, then. You know. You might need to call someone – not those useless idiots you hang around with." She wondered where 'those useless idiots' were. They were hardly his friends if they hadn't noticed his deterioration and done something to help him. She took her phone out of her back pocket and handed it to him to tap in his number. He paused before handing it back.

"What's that?" he asked. "A panther? Cool. Did you take that? Where, though? Not a zoo. Looks like England. It could be round here!" She looked. The background picture had defaulted to the photograph of the panther. The phone did that. She hadn't noticed. Ice began to tell Joe that it was a long story, but Buddy was beginning to make impatient complaining noises. He hadn't finished his walk and he was well-trained in some ways. He would never have messed in someone's garden. Before she could stop herself, she was allowing Joe to come with them and agreeing that she would relate it to him on the way.

Chapter 17 ~ Dragon

She told Joe all of it as they let Buddy run off the lead in the open patch of ground just up from the house. With the strange sensation of observing herself, she could hear that she was spilling out the whole tale, wondering why she was disclosing everything. Perhaps because she was not really interested in Joe's opinion of her. Or perhaps it was just the boy's quietness, his eyes focussed on Buddy trotting ahead. At one point she detected a slight 'tut' at the part where Daniel had gone to help the man in the lorry, and a little later Joe turned and looked at her with an amused raised eyebrow when she mentioned Marianne the witch-lady, but he made no comment. It was only when she described the panther in the road at Bale, that he let out a low, "Wow!" to show that he was impressed. When she finished, he merely said, "You do get around, don't you Ice?"

She nodded. She supposed she did. She liked the lonely places away from people. That usually took her off the well-beaten paths.

"But you know," he continued, "That place is bad news. You probably shouldn't hang about there too much – you never know what you might catch!"

"What? What place? What do you mean 'catch'?" Ice asked irritably, wondering if he meant the zoo. People did catch things from animals, that was true. Rabies and stuff. People were still suffering from the last virus that had infected nearly everybody and gone all around the world. A 'global pandemic'. That had come from wild animals originally – or so they said. She did not want to think that any of those animals in the cages had any diseases, and anyway, she hadn't touched them.

It was not the sort of thing that she would have thought of straight away though. She was more concerned *for* them than *by* them.

"That depot at Bale," he replied. "It's an arsenal, you know. It's a storage place for weapons. That's why they have those signs all over the place."

"Oh that! I know that. It's dangerous for the public, probably. They must have secure bunkers and things. They wouldn't want it all going off. I think they just don't like any random people wandering around if it's army land." She looked at him, waiting for him to expand on why she could catch something from being near a weapons base. She had a horrible feeling about what the explanation would be.

"Ice, it's always been more than just bombs and guns you know. The people who live round Bale used to write letters to the papers and go on TV. They've got nasty stuff there. Like chemicals and deadly things for biological warfare. But they don't say that because they're not supposed to. Like its a big agreement that nobody is allowed to use those things but everybody has them just in case and because they know the other guys do. Like nuclear weapons. MAD. Mutually assured destruction. They won't use them because you've got them and you won't use them because they've got them."

Ice did know about the nuclear stand-off. They had studied it in Year 7. Nobody had actually used an atomic bomb against an enemy since the Second World War, so it had apparently been successful. But people were afraid for decades that a crazy person would push the button. It had nearly happened a couple of times. Then there had also been attacks on nations who might be developing the bomb, to stop them from doing it, supposedly. Ironic, because the attacks had always been from nations that did have the bomb. Having nuclear weapons hadn't put a stop to wars.

Joe seemed surprisingly informed and she realised that she did not really know that much about this boy. Her encounters with him had mostly not been of the 'getting to know you' sort and her opinions had to keep shifting.

She felt that Joe was right about the chemicals – or was it biological materials? Diseases that could be released to kill whole populations. It was a hideous idea but it made absolute sense. That's exactly what the lorries were carrying – something toxic or the raw ingredients for a deadly weapon to be stored at the arsenal. They obviously did not want to broadcast that to the locals (or alert some unspecified enemy) and that's why there were no identifying features on the lorries – no hazard symbols or company names. And yet, there the lorries were at that site, actually just about visible from the road, depositing their lethal load into some secure storage for a purpose nobody would ever want to happen. Suddenly Ice had a horrible thought.

"Daniel!" she said out loud. Her head swam with alarm for her friend.

"Yeah. Not good," was Joe's reply.

She reached for her phone in her back pocket. She wished he would answer or reply to her text messages. She sent him another one. How was he? She was getting worried. Did he think he got contaminated by something in the lorry? Phone or text as soon as...

"That doesn't look too good either," Joe said suddenly, pointing.

The sky was darkening with the ominous signs of fires again. It looked like there were at least five different sources to the north and west of where they stood, the plumes of smoke billowing a mix of browns and greys against the blue. A wind was causing them to drift across the horizon and although Ice could not yet detect the acrid tang, Buddy barked a low 'wump' of warning. Ice gazed at the smoke, estimating the size of the fires and trying to calculate how far away they were. She didn't like the look of it. The fires were not near their houses but the number of plumes suggested they were spreading fast. They could easily be blown in this direction. There was no need to share all these thoughts; she turned to Joe and simply said, "We should go."

Ice bent to attach Buddy's lead and when she stood, she found the boy still staring past her, his mouth slightly open. She sighed and decided that she had better take him back to her house and feed him. Hunger was obviously making him slow and stupid.

"Wo!" Joe flicked his eyes fleetingly to Ice's face and then returned to gawp at the sky behind her. "That's what you were talking about, isn't it?" He was pointing.

She rotated to follow his indication. The smoke was still there, surging upwards and along from behind the trees and buildings, and there too, was another shape against the sky – a long, dark form, coiling and tracing serpentine patterns through the acrid clouds. This time there was no doubt – no breaking up into flights of birds. This was a creature of legend – an awesome leviathan, completely black apart from two flame-red eyes that glared out of an ancient, reptilian face. It raised its head and climbed high above the burning vegetation, circling over the top of the three observers, before turning back on itself and swooping down, weaving a spiral round its own long tail as it descended. Then it was gone, leaving no trace except for a faint trail where it had dragged a smoky path through the clouds.

It was not until they had reached Ice's house, half jogging, that they spoke.

"You saw it too?" she said. It was less of a question and more of a statement of astonishment.

"It was a bit bloody hard to miss, Ice!" Joe retorted. "Of course I saw it! What the actual… if you hadn't already told me about them… if you hadn't been there, I'd have thought I was hallucinating!"

He leaned over and put his hands on his knees. He was panting and looked ready to fall over with exhaustion. With a rush of guilt or compassion, Ice wasted no more time.

"Come!" she commanded.

There were tins of baked beans still in the cupboard. She tipped the entire contents of one into a bowl and heated it in the microwave before handing it to Joe who was seated at the kitchen table. There was no bread to make toast, but Joe did not complain. He bent over the bowl, gripped it in his right hand and with his left, spooned the mixture rapidly into his mouth, hardly chewing.

"Um… slow down a bit," Ice warned. "It's not good to overdo it on an empty stomach. You need to not rush or you'll cause yourself problems… you know… indigestion and… flatulence!"

Joe nodded, chewing more deliberately and with his mouth full, but he did not care and he did not reply.

Chapter 18 ~ Loss

It was Oscar who discovered that there was no water. They had stuck rigidly to their allotted time for turning on taps and filling containers, but now there was just a muddy sputter and then regardless of his waiting and annoyed grumble, nothing more.

Ice's mother returned to find the family gathered in the kitchen considering whether it was a local problem and wondering if it was related to the fires or was a more permanent issue. Joe had already left, saying he would check if there was any in his house and Ice had just received his text.

"Joe says he has no water either. He has some in bottles, but I've told him he can come here if he runs out. I hope that's OK. We have enough, don't we?"

Ice's mother nodded. She and Mr Cooper were exchanging looks and Ice felt as though a silent decision had been made.

"That's fine, Ice. I'm glad we stored some. We have enough for basic needs and a little to share if it comes to that," her father said. He was holding back again but Ice's mother did not.

"It's a bigger problem," she said. "They have started to evacuate people from the areas in the path of the fires. The road out of Depton was jam-packed. If they have no water on tap, they'll either have to truck or fly it in or probably – more likely now – just let the fires burn. Apparently, they're not heading in our direction, but still… things have a way of changing quickly these days. Perhaps we should get moving?" She shot a questioning glance at her husband. "Is it a risk to stay? At any rate, you two – it would be a good idea to be ready. Go and see that you've got what you need if we do have to leave suddenly – your bags. We'll shove the bedding in the car as well. Ice, help Oscar, would you? I will come and check in a minute. And don't worry – we'll be fine!"

Their mum looked at Oscar and smiled to reassure him. It did not work. Ice saw that his face had gone pale beneath his freckles and though he was trying not to, his expression gave away the rising panic.

"It's alright, Oscar," she said, as if by reassuring him she might quell her own feelings of dismay. "We've got our 'grab bags' remember? Let's go and compare notes. And yeah. Like mum says. Don't worry. I saw the fires. They're not coming this way. This is just a precaution. If we have to go, we'll all be together and it'll be an adventure!"

He looked unconvinced, but he did not cry and he followed Ice up the stairs. They would all be together. Ice had given the comforting words but in an unbidden thought, she contrasted her situation with Joe's. Completely on his own. Nobody to tell him what to do or where to go. How would he know? Would someone come round with a loudspeaker announcing the evacuation, like they did in the films? Could someone like Joe get away far enough and fast enough? Would there be something to pick people up? She imagined a truck full of Depton's strays – old people without cars, single mothers with new babies, abandoned teens…

The scene niggled her and she wished she could dispel the uncomfortable knot of anxiety in the pit of her stomach. Sorting things with Oscar, helped a little. It was good to focus on doing something practical and her little brother seemed to be channelling his fear into enthusiasm for the items that he had in his bag.

"This is a great thing," he said, showing Ice a coil of wire that could cut branches. "Look, it winds up really small and goes in here. And then I can make fires with this – not that we need to at the moment, but you never know!" He demonstrated by striking the two parts together and producing a spark that Ice was worried would set his duvet cover alight. "I've got more water and a bag of pasta and this tube of tomato paste. We'd have to be careful though. And if we need to we can boil any water that we find so that it would kill bacteria and things. We will find more water, won't we?"

Ice nodded. It was good that he was distracted by the thought of future dinners, but she knew he was scared. And he was right to be. She was, too.

It did not take them long and in the brief hiatus that followed, Oscar lay on his bed with his tablet. Ice left him immersed in a cyber world that at least he could control. She sent texts to Mia and to Daniel. Were they OK? Did they have water? What were they going to do? Mia's text came back almost instantly. She was fine. She wanted to see Ice. She would come round in a little while.

There was no text from Daniel. Ice hated using the phone to make actual calls. It was like disturbing people. They might be busy or it might be inconvenient. Then you had to think of what to say and to know when to terminate the conversation. It was much easier to text, but she was about to press the icon to dial his number when her phone began to ring. She was momentarily taken aback, but glad. The incoming call was from Daniel.

"Hey!" she said. "I was just going to call you! How are you? I was worried!"

"Ice," came a woman's voice on the other end. "This is Anna. Daniel's mother."

"Oh!" Ice's voice showed her surprise. "Hi. Is Daniel, OK?"

There was a pause. Ice could hear Mrs King taking a deep breath before replying, "We've lost him, Ice."

"What do you mean? Where did he go?" she said. It was not a good time to be wandering about the Warwickshire countryside, particularly if he was not very well. Ice had visions of Daniel being trapped by the fires somewhere. Why would he have left without his phone? That was silly! Had the illness made him delirious?

"Are they looking for him? Did you tell the police?" It was a standard question, though she thought about how the police had not been much help when her family had been looking for her mother last year – but maybe because Daniel was young, and it was dangerous, they might have a helicopter search. They did that sometimes, up and down the river when someone had gone missing. In case they had fallen in. Or they used to. She couldn't remember hearing the chopper recently. There was a muffled sound at the other end of the line.

"No, Ice. He hasn't gone missing." Mrs King's voice sounded odd. She was speaking in short broken sentences, gaps between the words. Ice could feel a cold sensation welling up from the pit of her stomach. "Ice…" There was another, longer pause and then she said, "Daniel died. This morning." Mrs King was openly weeping now, but she continued, as if she felt she had to explain. "He wasn't well – you know… but it seemed like a bout of the 'flu. He's had it before. He always shakes these things off. Last night he looked like he was… he was a bit better. Just sleepy. But this morning… he wouldn't…

I couldn't wake him. I... the ambulance took so long... he... slipped away before we got to the hospital. They tried... In the ambulance... They couldn't bring him back. I should have done something... sooner. But the doctor just said plenty of liquids and bed rest... Ice? Are you still there?"

Ice had not moved. Her mobile phone was still held against her ear but the roaring was all in her head so that she was surprised that she could hear the words that came from her mouth.

"Yes. I'm so sorry. Thank you for letting me know." So formal. Like an unsuccessful job application. From below her ribs there was a crushing pain that spread like a fire up through her chest. The walls of the room seemed to waver and vibrate and all she could do was to sink to her knees beside the bed and grip the covers with both hands, burying her face and gathering up the dense fabric and pressing it on either side of her head till it hurt. Sound and light from outside were obliterated, but she could not hide from the fury that was exploding inside. Fury at Daniel for never being able to take that ride with her. Fury at the truck driver for crashing with his toxic load. Fury at everybody for being so stupid that they could not stop themselves from making their own planet uninhabitable.

She wasn't sure how long she had stayed like that, immobile while the anger pounded and she screamed silently into the mattress. It had finally settled into a dull rage verging on numbness when she became aware that someone was in her room and then Oscar's gentle hand on her shoulder.

"Ice, what's wrong? What are you doing? Your friend is downstairs."

Mia was standing in the hallway looking up at her, as Ice, moving like an automaton, descended step by step. The two girls did not speak but each knew the other's pain, and as she caught sight of her friend, Mia's face crumpled and she cried, wiping the tears roughly with the back of her hand. The burning feeling in Ice's chest intensified but her expression was closed, even as she reached Mia and the two girls wrapped their arms around each other. They stood like that in the hallway, neither wanting to move away for the knowledge of the gap that had opened in both their lives. Finally, it was Mrs Cooper's voice that broke through and they dropped their embrace and turned to her.

"Whatever is the matter, girls? What's happened? Mia, are you OK? What's wrong?"

Mia began to sob again and Ice's mother instinctively came to give her a hug for comfort, looking over at Ice's stony face and silently requesting an explanation. Ice could hear herself telling the story in a flat, monotonous voice that did not reflect the feeling inside, and then she saw her mother's tears well up in sympathy for the two children who had lost a friend and for the mother who had lost a child. Mrs Cooper pulled Ice into the hug and the three of them remained like that together, while she said, "I'm so sorry. That poor boy!"

Eventually, there was a knock on the door and they broke away to let Mrs Cooper answer it, just as Mia said that it would be Kiran, her sister.

"Ice, I've got to go," she said, looking down. Kiran was on the doorstep and there was a large car by the kerb, heavily loaded, motor still running. From the passenger side, Mia's mum gave a brief wave but she did not smile or get out.

"You're leaving," Ice said, blankly. Mia nodded silently and then reached out and took Ice's hands in her own.

"We have to – we have no choice – and you should too. It's not safe here any more. I will find a way to keep in touch. I've got your number. I will send you my contact details as soon as I know where I am. We can video chat..." She began to cry again and quickly turned away, almost running so that she was inside and hidden by the baggage before her sister had reached the car. Mrs Cooper and Ice watched as it sped away from their house and away from Depton.

Chapter 19 ~ Plan

Ice was aware after that, of her mother's kindness. She was led into the kitchen and sat on a stool while her mother made some tea – the English panacea for all ills – and she was grateful just to have the warm cup – something solid to grip and focus on. At some point they were joined by her father.

"Oscar's asleep," he said. "It's not a bad idea and you might want to grab some before we leave. You can kip in the car, of course, but it won't be as comfortable! I've got some things to sort out. I've managed to find our rack for the roof and I've got to attach the trailer. A couple of hours at the most and then we should probably get going."

Ice shook her head.

"I'm not sleeping. Shouldn't we do something?"

"About what, Ice?" Mr Cooper asked.

Where to begin? There were the animals on the farm that would be burned to death in their cages if nobody was there to rescue them. There was stupid Joe in his house alone. There was Mrs King, grieving her lost son who had effectively been killed by the people at the weapons base at Bale. As powerful as they might seem to be, surely they had to be held to account for that? People should at least know.

She wanted to say all this to her parents and get their answers but she knew there weren't any that would be satisfactory. Instead, she simply replied, "We have to take Joe with us." She hoped they would understand the reasons without a long explanation. She was breaking her promise to him to not tell any adults.

Both parents looked at her. Ice met their gaze in silence. She knew they were working out what she meant, weighing up how much space he would take, how much food and water. They were thinking how he was not really their responsibility and considering whether another passenger would slow them down. Then her mother gave a brief nod.

"We'll find room," she said.

***

Two hours, her father had said. She thought about this, standing in the middle of her room staring at the blank screen of the computer. It would have to stay, of course. There was no point in taking that clunky old thing with them, though it had been a kind of friend over the past couple of years. She imagined what would happen to it if the flames reached their home while they were gone: an image of the plastic bubbling and melting and then of the screen exploding with the heat and showering the room with glass. A sad, if dramatic end for the old workhorse. Even if the fire did not come, Ice wondered when, if ever, they would return to this place.

"I was dreaming," Oscar said, interrupting her thoughts. He stood in her doorway, hair tousled and rubbing his eyes in the way people do when they are still feeling bleary from sleep. "It was very weird. Daniel was in it." He came into the room, sat on her bed and began tracing the pattern on her duvet absent-mindedly with his finger. "I liked him," he added sadly. "He showed me how to play NetHack on my phone. Young people shouldn't have to die."

"No," Ice agreed.

"In my dream, Daniel was standing outside. Not somewhere I knew but like a school field or something because there were trees in the background. I don't know why

I was there because I was in my pyjamas and was worrying about where I had put my shoes. I was scared my feet were going to get burned if the fires came. Then suddenly I was holding out my phone and asking if he thought I should be a Caveman or a Knight. He was saying something like, 'The great beasts are calling. The animals… something about them being a danger.' and, 'Tell Ice to go to or Bacon or something…' I don't know. It sounded familiar in my dream but I can't think of a place like that in real life. I've heard of Kevin Bacon. Maybe I was just hungry."

Ice was listening with interest, her eyes wide and focussed on her little brother.

"Dreams are weird," she said. She was controlling the emotion but could not completely disguise the trembling in her voice. "It's common for people to see someone who's died – you're thinking about them a lot and your brain conjures them up."

Oscar shrugged miserably and said, "S'pose so. But anyway. I thought you'd want to know. Dream Daniel seemed very sure that I had to tell you, so I've done that now." He made no effort to contain the tears that fell and he cried silently. Ice felt for her little brother but she was not going to cry now, herself. A cold fury was driving her to do something. She understood Daniel's message – if that was what it was. It was not that the animals were *a danger* – it was that they were *in danger*. And it was Baycote. She knew this because she had read something online about it recently. It was an area that had been fenced off to prevent wild swimming. The reservoir was an old clay pit that had supplied the local brick industry right up to the 1930s. Afterwards it had been left to become a wildlife habitat. Several weeks into the drought, she had seen a news item about water shortages. The quarry lake was down to half its normal level but some local teenagers had been caught trying to break in. It was surrounded by scruffy woodland planted in the last century, which had been allowed to grow largely untended for four decades. She could see why it would be a good place to release the animals. In the middle of the reservoir was a sizeable island – or nearly – just joined to the shore by a narrow strip of land. Here the animals would be as safe as possible. Still enough water to be protected from the fires but with a route to the main shore if they needed it. There were probably fish in the reservoir and abundant rodents and mallards. The fence would stop them from roaming freely to be killed on the roads or shot by farmers. Ice judged that most people had other things on their minds right now, but if the animals ever did need to be recaptured, it was a contained area, large though it was. It was a good place but it was roughly twenty miles away in the opposite direction to Bale. How on earth could she get the animals there and be back within two hours?

She did have a plan. Or part of one. Ice could not quite articulate the other part, yet. She needed some items from the tool box. And Joe's help.

Chapter 20 ~ Farm

"You haven't got anything ready to leave." Ice said to Joe, when he opened the door and she could see he had no rucksack or bags anywhere in case of emergency evacuation. Most people had that these days but it was just another way in which Joe's mother seemed to have let him down. He gave no response but stood back to admit Ice to the dingy interior again. She cut to the point.

"We're going, Joe! Evacuating. The fires are no longer being controlled and my parents are worried. You must come with us. Bring anything you can." She knew even whilst she said it, that Joe had little to bring. But he had water. He could put a couple of bottles in a bag at the very least. And some spare clothes or something. He did not seem to be responding very quickly and she needed him to get moving.

"Joe, listen. Do you have a bag to carry stuff?" He nodded and pointed at the school rucksack that was lying on the floor by the sofa. It was battered, but it would have to do.

"OK. Good. Pack those bottles and get some clothes and anything else you think you could do with on a journey. Like you're going away for a few days." She was directing him now. His face was ghostly in the gloom, the late afternoon sunlight barely filtering through the drawn curtains. He moved like a ghost too, obeying Ice without objection but without much sense of urgency, either. Ice stopped him with a hand as he made for the kitchen behind her.

"Before you do that, I want to ask you something. That van. The one that was left by your mum's... you know. The one in the garage out back. Is there any chance it can drive?"

The question seemed to reanimate him as Joe began to follow the direction of Ice's thoughts.

"Yes! Well it might, I mean. A couple of weeks ago when Gary was trying to get rid of it, some guys came round and he started it up for them. They didn't want it. It was too far gone. You know. The bodywork. There's loads of rust. And who wants diesel any more? They made him an offer for the battery and the tyres, but he obviously thought it wasn't enough because they left and that's why it's still there. It's completely illegal. No tax or MOT. What do you want to do? I can drive – I mean, I don't have a licence yet but I've driven before. And I know where he left the keys!"

Ice nodded.

"Get them. Get packed. I'll tell you on the way."

***

It had coughed a bit and taken two stuttering turns of the key, but the van had started. Thank goodness for the battery that the Gary person had been too stingy to sell! Ice was deeply sceptical about Joe's driving abilities and she knew that they were breaking the law in so many ways but the smouldering fury inside her had obliterated her concern. If they got caught, so what? Caught by whom, anyway? Police cuts had hit hard. The meagre number of officers that were employed in Warwickshire probably had enough on their plate dealing with the fires and the evacuation. She felt a little more guilty when she thought of her parents preparing at home and possibly wondering where she was by now. It prompted her to send a text message to Oscar who was the most likely to pick it up.

She was just fetching Joe. She wouldn't be long. It wasn't a complete lie – it just left out certain key details.

The boy beside her seemed happier than he had for a long while. His pathetically small bundle was stowed under her seat next to her bag of tools and he was almost smiling as they rolled along the road towards Bale. He was at home behind the wheel, she could tell. So many things in Joe's life had been outside his control – it must have felt good to be in command of something for a change.

He hadn't blinked at her plan either. He had simply pulled a kind of 'meh' face, and shrugged his shoulders, saying, "Yeah, OK. Let's do it." There were times when a reckless personality and contempt for authority had its advantages. Ice couldn't think of anybody else who would have just gone along and not tried to talk some sense into her. She was almost tempted to tell him the whole plan, but held back. She remembered his warning about the site at Bale and so she kept the second part to herself.

She checked her watch as they reached the turning for the farm. Just gone five. Time still to fit everything in and be home before they were due to leave. The sun was now below the horizon but the sky was still lit with a deep ochre visible in the south west as they drove towards it. More disturbingly, behind them the northern sky was now crimson and Ice had to fight back a surge of panic. The flames were clearly spreading quickly. From the direction of the smoke it looked like the wind was fanning them southwards and there was already the unmistakable tang in the air as Joe turned up the road to the farm.

"Here!" Ice shouted, causing Joe to brake a little sharply and pull the van to a rumbling stop by the road. The ponies were wild-eyed and skittish and whinnied as Ice jumped down and went to the farm gate. They could see and smell the approaching fires but their instinct to run was obstructed by the fence and the hedgerow. She cursed inwardly. The farmer had not moved them out of danger yet and they were too big for the van. On the strength of this it was very unlikely that the other animals had been made safe.

As she pondered what to do about them, the farmer appeared from behind the house in an overblown four-wheel-drive SUV of the kind supposedly designed for rough terrain. The vehicle pulled up at the gate and the occupant clambered out, leaving the car door open and the engine running. Though the dusk light had faded, the fires were bathing the sky in an orange glow, so that Ice was able to see the farmer. It was a woman, large framed and wearing the androgynous clothing of the farm – shirt, trousers, boots – possibly in her forties, with greying, close-cropped hair. On the passenger side, was the clearly recognisable silhouette of a dog – a collie type – border, most likely.

"What do you want?" she shouted at the two teens. "Why have you stopped here?"

Ice did not want to admit that she had been the one investigating the exotic pet collection earlier and the farmer gave no indication that she recognised her.

"We were worried about the ponies," she said. "We saw that they were getting scared. We wondered if they were going to be moved because of the fires. She pointed in the direction of the amber glow.

The farmer shook her head.

"You should not be here and I don't see how it is any of your business. I have more pressing concerns right now, with my sheep in the bottom field. The ponies will have to wait. I can't do everything. I will see to them and the others as soon as I can."

"Can we help? Can we do anything?" Joe asked. Ice could not see what they could do. Again the farmer shook her head.

"You can help by letting me get on with doing my job. I will be back for the horses when I've moved the sheep away from the fire. God knows if it will be enough! Now can you leave my property please?"

The two youngsters stood back to let the farmer through. Ice made a show of shutting the gate for her so that she did not have to get back out of the car before she drove off. she knew that the farmer was not lying. It was true that she was rushing to save the sheep if she could and that she intended to return afterwards, but Ice also knew that this would not happen in time.

As if to prove her judgement correct, the air was suddenly filled with stinging red embers that were blown about the two of them and the ponies, who became frantic. One of the terrified animals whinnied and reared up like a horse in a western film. At the other end of the field, dry vegetation caught and went up in flames, adding a brighter glow to the orange sky. The grass of the field was like tinder lit by the swirling debris blown from the burning trees and hedgerows behind, and it was obvious that the house itself was in danger.

"What do we do?" Joe shouted, coughing and wiping his eyes that were now streaming because of the stinging smoke. "Are we all going to die?"

"We're not going to die, Joe!" Ice replied. It was odd. Had she been on her own, she was sure she would have felt panic and desperation, but the presence of another human and the animals had forced her to take charge. They had very few options – the decisions were not that difficult to make.

"We have to let the ponies out on to the road. It's their only chance. If we leave them here they'll be killed by the smoke or burn to death. Or hurt themselves trying to get out. At least on the road they can head away from the flames and maybe find the river. I'll open the gate to their field – Joe, you drive up to the house. See if anyone is still at home and wait for me to help you load the cages."

As though aware of Ice's intentions, the ponies were ahead of her and already crowding by their gate when Ice reached it. The dry hedgerow around the paddock was like a fuse, providing a chain of fuel from one end to the other. Ice remembered Oscar's amazement at how quickly the tree had caught alight and how high the flames had leapt. The instant she opened the gate, the ponies pushed through and left at a canter, down the road in the only direction that was left to them away from the terror. She was relieved that they had seemed to understand which way to go, and hoped it would remain a safe route long enough for them to get to a fire-free refuge zone.

As she ran up the drive, she could hear Joe banging on the farmhouse door and shouting for anyone inside. He shook his head as he jogged down to the cages to meet her.

"Nobody's answering!" he shouted. "What now?"

Ice pointed to the cages. They were large enough to present a problem to a single person trying to lift, but between them, she and Joe could just manage. She had brought bolt-cutters and a fret-saw in case she had to cut through wood or metal, but in the end, neither was necessary. The cages were resting on stands that were little more than rough tables. They were not fixed down, relying on their shape and weight to keep in position.

"This one!" she shouted to Joe, lifting what looked the lightest, housing the three macaws. She contemplated releasing them there and then, using the bolt-cutters, but if they could be transported to a place of greater safety, they'd have more chance of survival. It was harder than it looked. The sharp corners of the wood cut into their fingers as they lifted and the birds inside flapped against the netting, throwing the two teens off balance so that they nearly dropped the cage. They half staggered to the open back door of the van and slid in the wooden structure until it came to rest against one of the wheel arches inside. The others were surprisingly less difficult. Unlike the birds, the mammals froze at the feeling of movement making their cages easier to lift and carry.

By the time they had finished loading, the sweat of the exertion had made rivulets through the soot that now covered both their faces and they were coughing with the effort of breathing the acrid air. Joe flapped his hand and put his thumb in his mouth.

"Ow! Little bugger bit me!" he complained without clarification. "Ungrateful or what?" He looked at Ice in the orange light of the approaching fires. She did not seem amused nor overly concerned about his finger. "Don't worry – I can still drive!" he said.

Chapter 21 ~ Trespass

She had to tell him now. He was already pushing in the clutch and letting the vehicle roll down the drive towards the gate.

"No – not that way. Not yet," Ice said, putting a hand on his arm as he made to turn left. There's something I want to do up here. She indicated the right hand direction. Joe raised his eyebrows, looking aghast.

"What? We've got to get going and take these little guys out of here!" he answered. "This way. Look!" He pointed to the fires that had spread to the farm outhouses. Ice felt a lurch in the pit of her stomach. It was a lurid scene – the dark smoke rolling against a backdrop the colour of pumpkin. But the fire had yet to reach the hedges on their side of the roadway and the other fields were still completely clear of smoke and flames. Working with Joe to get the animals loaded had provided a distraction, but the fury inside her still pushed her on.

"No – this way. To the MOD entrance. Take me to the gate and pull in just off the road. Then stay in the van and wait for me. I won't be long."

"Ice! Have you gone crazy? What the hell are you thinking? You can't go in there. Not now. Not ever. Let's take the van and get out of here." Joe's voice had a distinct edge of panic but Ice was unswayed.

"Now, please," she answered, firmly. "While we still have time." She couldn't tell him why she felt compelled to return. She didn't really know, herself. It was something about Daniel, but it was also the great beasts. The picture of the bear had confirmed it for her – it was somewhere she was meant to go, though she wasn't sure what she was supposed to find.

Joe shook his head and closed his eyes, audibly sighing, but he did as she asked and dragged the steering wheel down to the right. When Ice tapped on the windscreen and said, "There!" he pulled in sharply and drew the van to a halt off the road, a few metres away from the gate.

"Bring it round and wait for me. I promise I'll be quick. I'm just going to take some pictures. Then we can get those animals to Baycote. The reservoir. You know where that is?"

Joe nodded miserably. He looked like the last thing he wanted to do was to be stuck in a van in the middle of nowhere with a bunch of stolen wild animals while the countryside burned around him.

For now though, they had left the flames behind. From where she stood, next to the fence, Ice looked back the way they had come. She could not see the farmhouse across and down the road, but the night sky was bright with fresh fires and she was sure the main building had just caught alight. The rescue had been just in time.

It was surprisingly easy to slip into the grounds. The first gate was a low metal one with rusty, horizontal bars that Ice used as rungs, swinging her leg over the top and jumping down the other side. The razor wire fence looked forbidding, but it had clearly not been maintained very well; some animal had undermined it with a burrow that a skinny and determined teenager could squeeze through. She found herself brushing off the dry dust on a crude roadway that was little more than two uneven strips of tarmac.

The wind direction gave a temporary reprieve from the worst of the smoke which rose high into the sky, under-lit by the flames, but the air was still full of the smell of scorched things. What should have been a bright full moon was obscured, and a haze lay over everything. Trees and man-made structures loomed out of it, eerily lit in shades of orange. Lights which normally would have shone white from within their metal cages, emitted a sulphurous glow from the walls of the buildings and from four tall posts around the compound. Ice did not have the cover of darkness but it looked deserted.

From this position, the place where she had previously seen the lorries was obscured with tall conifers of some kind. Mentally, she mapped out the direction from her memory of peering through the hedge. The smoke was disorientating and made it difficult to see more than a few hundred yards. Holding her T-shirt over her nose and mouth with one hand, phone in the other, Ice made a crouching lope in the direction she thought was towards the parked vehicles. To her left, the squat tops of bunkers could be seen rising from the earth like ancient burial mounds. Still running, she turned briefly to look back the way she had come and with a sudden flush of horror, saw that the gate was no longer visible behind the thickening pall of smoke. The fires must have spread nearby. But she was compelled to look further and so she turned back, instantly colliding with something in her way.

Strong hands gripped her arms on either side and she heard a male voice. Ice looked up to meet the dark, angry face of the speaker. He was uniformed, but not with any military clothing that Ice recognised. He looked more like the security guard of an American shopping mall. He was frowning and demanding to know who she was and what she thought she was playing at. He seemed agitated and cross – and with good reason. It was not a place for teenage girls to be wandering around at the best of times.

Ice had no words for him that would matter. She struggled to break free but this only made him move his grip. With one hand, he held her left wrist, encircling it with an unshakeable clasp, like a steel manacle, and with the other, he wrenched her phone away, glancing at it briefly before putting it in a trouser pocket.

It was all Ice could do to not fight – to stop herself from hitting and kicking in the instinct to escape. But she held it in. It was not so much that she remembered her vow against violence but more that she knew it was futile. Struggling would make him tighten his grip. Fighting would enrage him further. She had little option but to allow herself to be pulled along roughly by the arm.

"You need to come with me and explain yourself!" he said. "Not only are you trespassing on private property – but in case you hadn't noticed, we're in middle of a f... in the middle of a flaming disaster. look around you! Are you completely stupid, or something? How did you get in here? Are there any others?"

Ice shook her head but remained silent. There was no point in roping Joe into this. Joe! Damn! He'd be waiting and wondering where she was. What was this man going to do with her? How long would it take? Joe couldn't wait much longer. She had already put him in enough danger. She had to get her phone back and get word to him to leave.

The grip on her wrist was painful now and Ice was having to jog to keep up with fast strides towards a white, concrete cuboid of a building. Though she stood passively, the guard continued to hold on to her like she might make a break for it, while he selected a key from a bunch that had been clipped to his belt, and unlocked the grey metal door. Ice was dragged into a small vestibule, no more than two metres square, and pushed up against the plain concrete wall while the guard shut and locked the outside door behind him before holding up his ID card against an electronic panel. At the top of this, an LED lit green with an accompanying beep and Ice could hear a lock click open.

Chapter 22 ~ Bunker

The room was like a metal box inside the concrete structure. On all sides, various fixtures jutted from the smooth, lime-green surfaces of the walls. There were pipes that obviously ran electrical cables to boxes which must have enclosed switches or power junctions, and a crude metal bookcase housed some stubby red and blue files. Three sides had waist-high steel cabinets topped with wide work surfaces and on the walls just above these, were many plug sockets some with attached devices. Most of these were unfamiliar to Ice, but she recognised a pair of old-style walkie-talkies next to a black box. Across the end workbench, a bank of five computer screens were lit with views of the grounds, maps, and what looked like virtual control panels. At one of the computers, a woman stood, occupied with the mouse and with typing something rapidly into the keyboard. She was wearing a headset and was talking urgently to someone on the other end.

"…And I am telling you that it has moved out of zones! You gave me assurances… No, I cannot! I have to close down… no I already evacuate the whole site! It is completely predictable – No! I told you I leave now. We must hope…"

She stopped abruptly mid-sentence, staring them in astonishment, as the security guard entered dragging Ice forward and pushing her into the middle of the room.

"I found this one on the premises," he said before the woman had recovered her voice. Ice rubbed her wrist where he had released his hold.

The woman was wearing the plain clothes of an office worker – black trousers and a pale blue shirt, the sleeves of which were rolled up to her elbows. It was not a good choice of fabric: dark sweat patches were clearly visible in the armpits and even with the air-conditioning which filled the room with a low hum, she looked hot and flustered. Her hair was roughly tied up but damp strands had escaped and been irritably pushed back from her face. Ice was not good at guessing ages but she knew she couldn't have been much older than thirty. On a lanyard round her neck, was a plastic ID card, the name not visible to Ice. Temporarily, the woman seemed stunned with disbelief at Ice's presence. She stared at her, the computer mouse still held aloft as though she had been frozen in the moment of action, and then she spoke.

"Oh my God! Who are you and what are you possibly doing here?" There was a slight accent. Eastern European or Russian, Ice thought. "Is this some kind of teenage messing about? Because you are in a lot of trouble. This is restricted area. Did you not read signs at the gate? What are your parents thinking, letting you out at a dangerous time?" She turned to the guard and nodded as though implying that she would take over with Ice now.

"Thank you, Andrew. I am nearly finished here. Go! I will be right behind you."

He hesitated briefly and seemed about to say something but was forestalled by a louder and more urgent command from the woman to hurry up. He shrugged and placed Ice's phone on the work surface before leaving quickly.

"I have not time for this!" the young woman shouted at Ice. "Everyone has evacuated the site already and I am leaving now. You need to come with me. Are you alone? What are you doing here?"

Ice nodded her reply. She wasn't going to let on about Joe. She stepped forward and surreptitiously palmed her phone when the woman momentarily turned away to the computer. It was just enough time for Ice to photograph the screens before slipping it into her shorts pocket.

"I came to see," Ice said, blankly, even though she was conscious of how uncomfortably her heart was thumping in her chest. She was in trouble but *they* were the guilty ones – not her!

The woman shut down the computers and flicked some switches on the wall before turning back to Ice with a terse, "What?"

"The lorries." Ice replied. "I wanted to see them and where they put their contents. Storing the poison on this site somewhere. So I can tell people what the army is doing here. They're making chemical or biological weapons aren't they? I know what it is. What you're doing. You killed my friend, Daniel!"

The woman stared at Ice, brows furrowed, mouth slightly open. A mixture of extreme annoyance and confusion. When she spoke, it was as though she were addressing a stupid child.

"You have no idea what you are talking about… you seem to have some pretty strange ideas, young lady… what is your name?"

"Sarah," Ice replied. It was the first name that came to mind. She was not about to give her own. She felt a buzz against her right thigh. It would be Joe calling her. Or her mother perhaps! How long had she been? It was important now to get out of this place and back to Depton.

"This is lot of nonsense, Sarah!" the woman repeated, now with Ice's fake name for emphasis. "We are not military base. Not for long time. It is private company." She steered Ice towards the door. "Come we need to go. I must take you with me – I cannot leave you."

As if to prove her point, clouds of smoke rolled in through the newly opened external door and both Ice and the woman coughed and covered their faces with the fabric of their shirts.

"Move!" she shouted and Ice had little alternative but to run after the woman who was now making a low sprint towards a car-shaped blob which emerged from the smoke as they got closer.

The car was new, fully electric and well-sealed. Inside, there was a reprieve from the toxic air, though they both continued to cough and wipe their eyes. Smoke was the biggest danger in a fire, Ice reminded herself and wondered briefly if they would be able to get out of it or die here and be found later as just two charred corpses in the burnt-out wreck. She felt the phone in her pocket. Could she risk using it?

"I need to call my mum," she said. It wasn't a lie. She did need to call her mum, but it wasn't who she was about to call. She wondered if the explanation was enough or if the woman would confiscate the phone. But she was distracted – busy starting the motor and putting information into the SatNav, and not listening to Ice, anyway.

"Hi, it's me," she said quietly as Joe answered, and then more loudly, to cover the sound of his panicky response, "I'm fine! It's OK. I'm with someone now and we're in a car. Yes. We're going to evacuate this place. You must go. Do the… thing… with the you know… and I will meet you at home. Yes, I promise. No. Um tell… Dad I'll be there soon!"

She had no idea if the woman would be willing to take her to Depton, but she had to get Joe out of Bale. Wherever they were going, she would contact her parents to fetch her. She did not relish the thought of their reaction.

The car took a different route out of the compound to the one Ice had used entering it. This was another set of gates which must have locked electronically because the woman pulled up and wound down the window just enough to hold a card up to a machine, causing the gates to swing out automatically. Once they were through, Ice looked back to see if they closed on their own behind them, but they were already obscured by the yellow-brown haze.

"What is this story you were telling me about your friend?" the woman said suddenly, as they made their way on the road away from the compound. It was hard driving. At times there were clear patches, as the smoke drifted unevenly across the countryside. Then the woman would accelerate only to have to slow down suddenly in denser parts where the roadway could not be seen. Ice had no idea where they were going, but she had no choice but to sit there and hope that the woman knew what she was doing. The SatNav on the dashboard showed a large blue arrow on a winding road. At least they were moving away from Bale.

"Your chemicals killed him," she replied bluntly. "That stuff in the lorry. When it crashed, we were there. Daniel helped your driver but he cut himself on the metal and got sick. He was poisoned wasn't he? They thought it was just a virus but then he didn't get better. There was a big hazard clear-up operation that day. What are you storing? Everyone should be told. It's dangerous. You're killing people."

Ice could hear herself talking. It sounded ludicrous. Tin-foil hat stuff.

The woman was shaking her head.

"I am sorry about your friend," she replied, but you have made mistake. These are not the things in our storage facility."

She could not sense that the woman was lying, but there was a strong feeling that she was covering. There was guilt mixed in with annoyance.

"We are not keeping chemicals for this thing you are saying. This is not military. It is private company. It is for storing. Sometimes chemicals. Sometimes waste. We are renting old military property."

Ice listened in silence. She still had enough righteous anger to want to catch the woman in a lie. What she was being told sounded like the boring truth but not all the pieces fitted and Ice knew some bits were missing.

"So what *is* in there then?" she asked, "Because if it's nothing dangerous then why the hazard-taped clear-up? Why the need for such security? Why did the video disappear from my friend's phone?"

The woman shrugged and shook her head.

"It is not so toxic like you say. That chemical will not kill a person in that way – one little scratch. But still it is dangerous. Some is waste from industry – fuel and chemicals for operations. Some is not good to the environment and not to be breathed. It can hurt skin. Some is flammable. But it is not in the way you say. We handle it safely. It is unfortunate – the accident with the lorry but we deal with it quickly and nobody is hurt."

"Somebody was hurt! And why was our video mysteriously deleted?" Ice retorted. "And also why are those lorries unmarked and driving about the c..."

Ice did not have time to finish her questions, nor to receive any answers. As they approached the small tunnel beneath a railway bridge, the air was filled with a rain of fiery sparks coming from a great ash tree that was burning high on the embankment ahead. If she had slowed down just a little, the woman might have seen in time, the huge branch break away from the main trunk and tumble amidst a fountain of embers to land like a burning brand in the road just in front of them. If she had not been trying to press on – if she had not been distracted by Ice's questions, or confused by the smoke and the flames – she might have avoided what happened next.

Chapter 23 ~ Alone

Something was pushing down on Ice's head and she wondered if she had been hit by one of the falling branches. Her hair was around her face and she felt a constriction across her chest and legs where the straps of the seatbelt were pulled tight. Squinting through the shattered front windscreen she saw a world outside which looked wrong, and with a rush of realisation, she knew that she was upside down, pressed against the roof of the flipped car. She was still partly suspended by the seat-belt which she now scrabbled in a claustrophobic panic to unclip, releasing herself so that she fell into a clumsy crouch and banged her knees on the hard surface.

Stones and sharp, dry vegetation dug into Ice's palms as she groped her way round to the driver's side. Here, the roof had completely caved in. Although the sky was lit with the diffuse glow from the surrounding fires, the sun had long since set and it was hard to see inside the chassis. Using her phone as a torch, Ice peered in through the now open frame where the side window used to be; the woman seemed to be staring at her, eyes wide open, but her head was twisted at an impossible angle and there was no life in the gaze.

Fear and dismay flowed through Ice like a wave, making her head spin and causing her to dry heave as if she was about to vomit. She closed her eyes tightly and pulled her knees up to her chest, hands clasped over her head to make herself as small as possible and shut out everything she did not want to see and feel. She was aware of herself whimpering like a young animal, but there was nobody and nothing to hear her. She was alone and lost and in the middle of a conflagration.

How stupid she had been! Why had she built up a fantastical story about the lorries and about Daniel? She had made up a whole conspiracy, involving secret weapons and the military. Yes, it was nasty stuff that was being stored, but not biological weapons. 'It could hurt skin' the woman had said. Was that enough to have really harmed him or had Daniel just caught something naturally and been unlucky? Poor boy. It seemed that she had been spending too much time on her own, generating paranoid thoughts! Real explanations were often a lot more mundane and unexciting than we imagined.

Except things still niggled. Something was not right about that place. A *lot* was not right about any of it and Ice knew better than anyone that things could be weirder than most people imagined. Not everything was a fantasy. Even Joe had seen the dragon in the smoke. The arrival of the giant beasts – that was no coincidence was it? She had a strong feeling that they had been seen for a reason and that she had been 'drawn' to Bale. It wasn't the same as the shadelings before. Those dark, little creatures had literally shown her the way. These 'Old Ones' as Marianne had described them, had been much less direct about it, but she had still felt their intention, hadn't she?

The thought pulled her out of her self-pitying paralysis. Ice had to will herself to move or surviving the accident would be for nothing. In the beam of the headlights, she saw that there was a distinct layer of cleaner air below the swirling fumes. It was what she been taught by the fire-fighters who had visited her primary school years ago: the way to escape in a fire was to keep below the smoke-line.

Pulling herself back up to a low crouch, she summoned the courage to reach in through the driver's window, placing her fingers on the lifeless wrist, and confirming that there was no pulse. The woman's ID lay flat against the inside of the roof, the name now visible to Ice.

"I'm sorry, Elena Nicolescu," Ice said, out loud. Ice was sorry, too, that the car SatNav had been crushed beyond help. She reached in further to switch everything off and immediately thought better of it. It would feel like a final act but a pointless courtesy that would kill the headlights and plunge her into darkness. She thought of the inevitable fate of the car. The fires would reach here soon. It would be engulfed. The flammable parts would burn furiously, leaving very little trace of the occupant.

In any other circumstances, she knew that you were advised to stay by a site and not go wandering off. She had seen plenty of documentaries of people who had survived plane crashes or shipwrecks, only to die from thirst or exposure because they had become lost and had missed being rescued. But she had no choice. She did not know where she was, but she did know that it was not where she should be, and she was fully aware what it would mean if she stayed.

The tiny battery icon on her phone indicated thirty-five percent remaining power. Ice squinted at the map which lit up her screen. In night mode, roads showed up bright against a dark background. There was the railway line and the road they had travelled. The phone GPS was on, showing her approximate position somewhere inside a superimposed blue circle. For a moment, she felt a touch of hope that she could call for help. That somebody could rescue her. She pictured a helicopter lowering one of its long, dangling ladders for her to climb. Or her parents could find her if they knew where she was. She peered at the screen. Not even the tiniest of the grey bars was lit. Of course there wouldn't be any phone service!

Ice gave way to a moment of defeat and sat back on the hard earth. She knew which way to go – the slope of the ground and the map on her phone both pointed the direction to the river, such as it might still be after the long drought. However, it was becoming increasingly difficult to motivate herself to move. The air down here was not as smoky as the layer above, but it felt thick and warm and she wondered if she might be starting to suffer from the effects of carbon-monoxide poisoning – a subtle killer, lulling people into a stupor before suffocating them in their sleep.

"Don't go to sleep, then." It was like Daniel's teasing tone in her head, but it made her shake off the drowsiness and open her eyes. And then, reflected eerily bright in the beam of the headlights no further than a few quick paces, was another pair of eyes and the dark outline of a fellow living creature. Ice's breath caught in her throat. She felt a rush of gratitude for the unexpected company of the big cat, and a jolt of fear. She knew she was completely vulnerable if it decided to attack, but the animal acknowledged her presence only with a perfunctory hiss before sloping off.

It was what she needed to galvanise her. Half scrambling, half slipping, failing to avoid being scratched by the vegetation, Ice followed as quickly as possible, down the incline towards the safety of the water.

Chapter 24 ~ River

The drought had wrought its damage on the river, but it had not totally destroyed it. Wide, exposed flanks of mud were evidence of how far it had receded but through the middle, it still flowed, perhaps not much more than a metre at the deepest. For the creatures caught in the fire, the water offered the best chance of survival and Ice was not the only one that had instinctively sought it. She was conscious of the others: small shapes moving quickly past her; the slow flap of wings vibrating the air. It was comforting to think that this decision was at least shared. Not only was it the quenching element of water that would stop the fire in its tracks, but thousands of years of erosion had created the valley where there was now a layer of better air that meant Ice no longer needed to draw desperate breaths near the ground.

Risking the treacherous mud by the water's edge, Ice scooped up handfuls of the cool liquid and splashed it on her face and into her eyes, trying to remedy the effects of the acrid smoke. Though she was tempted to drink, she did not. Even with the overarching smell of burning, the rotten egg odour of decomposing vegetation was noticeable. It would be stupid to survive this, only to get sick later.

The current of clear air allowed her to look properly at her surroundings visible in the orange light for the first time since the crash. Plants near the water had been spared the flames, though the surface was bright with the reflection of fires which were burning further away and higher up. The banks were dotted with small boulders and debris that had been washed downstream, but it was a relief that there were no shopping trolleys or any of the other dangerous, human rubbish she was used to seeing in town.

She became aware of her lower legs sinking deep into the soft mud and though it was seductively cool, she did not want to become stuck. With some effort, she dragged them out, her arms clasped behind each knee in turn to pull against the sucking power. Instead of heading up the bank, she made her way into the water itself, where the riverbed was firmer underfoot. Even with the level as low as it was, the current was enough to make her unsteady. As she stepped, she could feel her legs being taken forward from under her and for a short while she found herself gliding down river in a seated position, sculling frantically with her hands to maintain equilibrium, and being bumped against the rocks beneath her. If the water had been just that little bit deeper, she might have made good progress like this – or even by moving to her front and adding in some swimming strokes – but the current was too slow and the rocks too painful.

Allowing herself to be pulled into a kneeling position, she clambered to her feet and moved away from the deepest part of the river to where it was still firm enough to stumble through the shallows without sinking into mud. It was hard going, nevertheless – difficult to see submerged obstacles, and several times, cursing, she slipped on the rounded surface of a boulder or tripped over the remnants of the water-lily roots. Fatigue was setting in but Ice was not quite ready to give up, following the flow of the water and her fellow creatures who were heading in the same direction.

At one point she looked up and was startled by the sight of two small deer standing midstream, their silhouettes stark against the water's bright surface. One stooped to drink and then raised its head suddenly, startled, ears flicking towards an unseen danger before they both bounded away abruptly.

Ice could see the source of their alarm. From the shaded bank opposite, a familiar shape emerged and crouched at the water's edge. It raised its head and she was sure that it was looking right at her. Its cat eyes were much better than her human ones in this light. She wondered what had delayed it. The Beast of Bale was so much more adapted to moving through this terrain than she was. The panther's pace should have taken it far ahead by now.

It was almost like finding an old friend in the devastation, and for a while she was spurred on, desperately trying to keep up and maintain her view of the lithe, dusky figure as it moved effortlessly ahead of her on the other side. Her progress was hampered by her tiredness and her clumsy human skills, so poorly evolved for trudging through uneven terrain strewn with obstacles. Yet somehow, she kept sight of the big cat, till she began to laugh inwardly at the thought that it was deliberately pacing itself to her pathetically slow progress. This impression was enhanced by the animal pausing on several occasions and turning to look back in Ice's direction. As far as she knew, panthers were solitary creatures, but maybe in the years of captivity it had become used to humans and in some way could feel the companionship as much as Ice did. Either that, or it was keeping her in sight as a potential source of food. She wasn't as quick as the deer.

"If I die, out here," she said aloud, "You're welcome to eat me!"

It was true, though she hoped it would not come to that just yet. They had made a fair amount of progress downstream since the car crash. At some point they would surely find a safer place, but every time Ice looked hopefully for the tell-tale darkness that would show a gap in the fires, she saw trees alight just beyond the edge where the land rose away from the river, and she did not have the courage to leave the safety of the water.

She had begun to entertain the mad thought that she would have to continue until she reached the sea, miles away and days of walking, when her journey was abruptly cut short. A few hundred yards in front of Ice on her side of the bank, was a centuries-old willow that had once trailed thin fronds in the water. Now it had caught fire and burned like a giant torch, roaring and crackling louder than the surrounding forest and sending flames and bright particles spiralling high into the air. The panther ahead of Ice quickened its pace suddenly and sprinted beyond the tree which had eclipsed everything downstream. Ice was not so fast. Stopped in her tracks by the size and intensity of the flames, she froze, heart pounding in her chest. She needed time to gather her wits, crouching down to drench herself in water – a meagre defence against the radiant heat scorching her skin – and then she began to move across the river, to the other bank, where she would follow in the panther's footsteps to make a run for it. But it was too late. The combined assault of the floods and the drought and now the fire had wrought its worst on the old tree. Ice ducked instinctively and covered her head as the great flaming trunk heaved over and came crashing down across the river in an explosion of sparks.

Chapter 25 ~ Dream

Now she really *was* ready to give up. The willow was a burning barricade that meant she could not continue downstream. Her companion was gone. She hoped he had made it to safety beyond the tree, but she had nowhere left to go. She had no idea whether or not she was completely hemmed in by the flames, but she knew she could not leave the river valley which provided the only pocket of relatively smoke-free air. She did not know how right she was. In places where the fire burned most fiercely, the air itself was superheated and one breath would have meant instant death.

Ice retreated upstream away from the intense radiance of the tree. Her only thought now was that she would have to sit it out in the river and wait for the fires to die down. She lay on her front in the water, submerging herself entirely before crawling to where a large boulder protruded from the riverbed, its smooth top just breaking the surface of the water. Here she sat cross-legged, pinned behind the rock, allowing the water to flow past her as though she were just another ancient, natural part of the landscape.

When she had been able to make her way down the river with the other animals, the adrenaline of the escape instinct had kept Ice going, but now her chance was gone and she felt the draining effects of fatigue. She wondered whether the oxygen was being used up by the fires and if it was that, along with the heat and the smoke she had breathed in, which was making it difficult for her to stay awake and focussed. She was aware of an overwhelming desire to close her eyes and drop her head down to rest it on the boulder. Ice tried to fight the urge, being not entirely sure that she would wake up if she fell into the water. It would be an ironic death, to drown in a forest fire.

Unconsciousness crept up unnoticed, fooling her into thinking that she was still awake, even as her musings drifted and became unreal. Her eyes closed and she sagged, head down. Thoughts turned to dreams populated with those familiar dense flocks of birds that wove their mesmerising patterns in the sky, transforming from giant beast to giant beast. Ice dreamt she was in the field with the ancient stone circle, standing below the amazing spectacle, looking up, a cool breeze blowing about her. In her sleeping state, the roar and crackle of the blaze became the cries of the huge animals who morphed between forms: the bear, the stag, the dragon and the magnificent black horse of her first sighting.

Dream Ice must have climbed or leaped or flown because suddenly she was on top of the tallest of the stones, reaching up to the sky like she was trying to catch hold of the horse. It was high, away from her grasp, but as though she was the narrator of her own dream script where the characters would bend to her will, the horse descended instantly out of the sky and landed at the far end of the field, long mane and tail billowing in the wind.

Ice tried to clamber down from her rocky perch and run to the horse, but her legs felt both immovable and ready to collapse at the same time. They buckled at the knee so that she tumbled from the stone and then found they would not support her. She was forced to crawl on the ground towards the creature while it stood and eyed her impassively. Beneath her clutching hands, the ground was soft and jelly-like. She could not find a purchase to drag herself forwards, though she made to grasp at the strange objects around her. At one point she came across a cloth bundle. As she grabbed it, the bundle wriggled, causing it to burst open and spill a swarm of small hedgehogs. These became tiny black creatures – miniature versions of the shadelings she had not seen for nearly two years. She felt an upsurge of happiness – like meeting some welcome companions – before they scattered in all directions and dissolved back into the ground where they belonged.

Unable to make any progress towards the horse, Ice was overwhelmed with the desire to curl up in a foetal position on the soft ground and, just like she was asleep in the real world, close her eyes and drift off.

"You probably shouldn't do that, Ice." Still in her dream, she opened her eyes and with a rush of relief, saw that it was Daniel crouched beside her, grinning and staring closely into her face. She smiled back at him, revelling in his apparent presence – he wasn't gone after all.

"You should wake up, actually," he said. "It's time to move."

Ice did not want to move. It was nice here at the stone circle with Daniel and the horse. She was comfortable and away from the river and the forest fire. The trees were lush and green, as they had been in the spring. If only the ground did not feel so unreal. If only she could feel or move her legs. If only she hadn't thought about those things. Disappointment and consciousness flooded back and she woke knowing that she was not safe in a spring field near Depton – she was in mortal peril in the middle of the Warwickshire countryside and her legs had indeed gone numb from her seated position by the stone.

She had yet to open her eyes. She knew what she would see and she did not want to be reminded that she was in for a long wait. For a while, she kept them closed, listening to the noise of the fires that burned nearby and feeling the movement of warm air. She was startled by a sudden short gust in her face and opened her eyes quickly. The shape of something she could not distinguish was directly in front of her, obscuring her view, and she fell back in fright, having to put her hands out behind to avoid plunging beneath the water. Semi-supine, and awestruck, Ice took measure of the shape and recognised it. That long dark nose ending bluntly in a soft muzzle showing two flared nostrils – the source of the sudden burst of air. A flowing mane gracing an elegant, dark neck. As the creature moved towards Ice, heavy hooves kicked plashes in the water. She felt frozen in place, even as the great horse lowered its head to hers, snorted gently and nudged her, staying so close she could have counted each one of the long lashes that fringed its huge eyes.

It was tempting to think that she was still asleep and dreaming, but Ice knew from the acrid air, the still blazing willow tree and the pins and needles in her legs, that this was real. The horse pushed her again so that she was compelled to scramble backwards before rising unsteadily to her feet, legs stiff and unbiddable. She was overwhelmed by the stunning beauty of the animal before her. It was the exact image of the horse she had seen in the flock of birds that day, long ago in school, but here it was a solid, natural thing with a glossy, black coat reflecting orange light from the fires. It seemed immensely tall. She had not had much experience with horses. Once she had ridden a pony at her primary school and even that fat little steed had felt dauntingly large at first. This creature would have towered above the pony, more than twice its size.

She was startled when the horse reared just enough to raise its hooves from the water and bring them down with a splash before turning its head away from her in the direction of the burning willow tree. Ice remained rooted to the spot, at a loss to know what to do. The horse approached her again, this time putting its head level with her stomach and giving her a sturdy shove that made her step back to keep her balance. It came forward once more, flanking her, pushing her to one side and circling, and then lowering its head to the water in front of her. Ice felt her pulse racing. She was nonplussed at the behaviour of the great creature and intimidated by its strength and size.

"What are you waiting for – a written invitation?"

It was Daniel's laugh and his voice in her head again – the same tone he always used to make light of a tense situation. She almost replied out loud. What was she expected to do? But the reply came to her with the realisation that it was crazy, just as the animal stooped to its knees beside her.

"Go on, Ice. Get on the horse, for goodness' sake!"

Chapter 26 ~ Ride

It was obviously what she was supposed to do because rather than shaking her off or biting, the horse allowed her to scramble on to its lowered neck. She had to use handfuls of the thick mane like a rope to pull herself up, and then she kept hold of these, twisting them round her clasped fists. It showed no objection to this indignity and seemed to approve because Ice had to tighten her grip, sliding backwards to a riding position, when it rose from its knees and with a quick turn, set off downstream.

The speed of the creature was terrifying and exhilarating. At first Ice clung on grimly, sure that she would be thrown off. As they approached the burning willow, the horse did not alter its pace or direction and she had little time to swear under her breath before they were off the ground, over the trunk, past the flames and down on the other side.

"A clear round!" was the teasing voice in her head, commenting on her show-jumping skills. The Daniel that she seemed to have conjured up was obviously finding this all very amusing.

With the obstacle of the willow left behind, Ice began to settle into her unexpected role as jockey. Though the situation was uncanny, the animal that she rode was very real. She could feel the power in the great shoulder muscles moving beneath her hands. When leaning forward, lowering her head to its neck, she inhaled the warm, mammalian odour and saw tiny rivulets of sweat on its dark coat. But though Ice had nothing with which to compare the pace of this ride, she felt sure that it was faster and smoother than it should have been, and with less contact with the ground. She was not going to complain.

With every second, the air grew clearer and the fires more distant. Her instincts and those of the animals that had been with her had been correct. The river flowed away from the strongest blazes, through areas that smouldered and then were extinguished, having already exhausted their fuel supply.

For a while they galloped on downstream and the countryside opened out on either side of the river, showing the fires receding. The sky was still bathed in an unnatural glow, but the smoke became thinner and another light was visible – the full moon, shining red through the high haze.

Ice did not know how far they had come, nor how long she had been riding but she was aware of the blessed relief of cooler air before the horse slowed its course along the river valley and veered to the right, mounting the bank on to a country road. Here, the journey came to an abrupt stop. Ice stayed seated on the broad back, wondering what to do next, while the creature stamped great hooves on the solid surface and exhaled noisily in the way that horses do.

Still clinging to its mane, Ice moved stiffly, and with some effort, leant forward and managed to wriggle her right leg over the horse's back to jump to the ground. It was an ungainly dismount. As her feet touched, there was no strength in her legs and when she unclasped her stiffened fingers, she collapsed to a seated position by the side of the road. Now that she was back on dry land, her shoes were uncomfortable and heavy with the river water. Ice rubbed the backs of her knees to try to persuade her legs to do their job and then rose unsteadily to a standing position.

The full moon shone more brightly here, no longer obscured by dense smoke, and it bathed the roadway and the two of them in its cold light. Ice gazed about her. It could have been any country lane in just about any English county. Opposite, dry hedgerows framed a small derelict field of ragweed, dried up dock and old cow parsley stalks. On this side, the verge rose steadily, so that a few metres ahead there was a high bank bordering the road.

"I have no idea where you've brought me, but thank you," she said quietly. The horse gave a brief toss of the head, allowing Ice to approach and place a tentative hand on the soft muzzle.

Doing so, she caught a movement in the brush just few metres ahead and then, almost as clear as the day she had first seen it, perfectly illuminated in the moonlight, the panther padded noiselessly on to the tarmac. It stopped in mid-step, catching sight of Ice and her companion who had seen it too. The great horse, head raised and ears flicked forward towards the newcomer, did not move from its spot, merely swishing its long tail and watching. For a moment, the two creatures eyed each other and then, as though there were some silent communication, the black cat turned away and bounded smoothly up the road and out of sight. It was wonderful to see it again. Her old friend. The Beast of Bale. It looked like they were both survivors.

The big cat had certainly appeared to know what it was doing and which direction to take, but Ice was not so sure. She glanced back at the horse. It had stooped its head as if to nibble at the vegetation by the verge. She wished she could have continued their speedy journey until they had reached somewhere familiar, but it looked like this was as far as her rescuer was prepared to take her. Even as that thought occurred to Ice, the great animal moved away from her a little, and then further, stepping into the deep shadows cast by the high bank until its dark shape almost disappeared in the gloom.

"Wait!" Ice's voice was harsh in the still air. The thought of being left again caused a wave of anxiety and she broke into a stumbling run to catch up. She could still hear the clopping of the giant hooves striking the roadway, but when she reached the shadows, the sound was already fading. And then there was quiet. Ice stared down the road, eyes wide, desperate, but unable to see the reassuring form. She forced herself to a painful sprint, though she knew by the time she was out of breath, that it was a hopeless chase.

The road was empty and lit only by the moon that was fast travelling across the sky. In a little while it might be difficult to see. Ice wondered if she would end up blundering about in the dark and how long it was till dawn. It was the combination of these thoughts that reminded her with a sudden pang of dismay that she still had her phone and that she had not thought to protect it from the water. With a sinking feeling, she reached into her pocket. The phone was dark and damp and Ice knew better than to try the screen. That was the best way to kill a wet phone. You were supposed to put it into dry rice or something.

"Do you happen to have any dry rice on you?" It was that cheeky voice again. If he wasn't going to be helpful, perhaps Daniel should keep quiet, Ice thought.

"OK," came the voice again, as though he was standing next to her. "Maybe try and dry it off. You know – open the back up. Wipe off the drips. Go on. It's worth a try, isn't it?"

It was what she was thinking anyway, as she dropped to a semi-crouch, back against the high bank for stability. Her fingers felt thick and far from nimble. She was aware of a sense of creeping brain-fog and tried to shake it off, concentrating on the steps of the procedure: fingernail under the back cover; prise it off; remove battery and card; dry them as well as possible using the edge of her T-shirt which was itself still damp; tap the phone to dislodge any lurking drips; wipe it all down again; replace everything and then…

What were the chances that the phone would work and still have enough charge to be useful?

"Well it's no use at all at the moment, is it?"

Ice shook her head and pressed and held the 'on' button, half expecting a spark and a catastrophic failure. When the well-known logo glimmered on the screen, she blessed the phone manufacturer for their robust product, and held her breath, waiting for the crucial seconds that would show whether it would live or die. The phone pinged, lighting up fully and providing the user with a prompt for a password. Ice stood up and out loud to nobody, gave a triumphant, "Yes!" that seemed to be echoed close by, along with the sound of a brief laugh.

Only seventeen percent of the battery power remained. It would have been enough to ring home or to send a text, but Ice kicked against the roadside bank in frustration. How was there still no phone service? Pushing down her disappointment, and even though she knew it would use up precious power, she opened the maps app. As before, she could see that GPS was active and working; the map zoomed in and the blue circle appeared to show her whereabouts.

The great horse had brought her to a remote area. Why had it done that? The nearest signs of habitation were miles away and these were the odd farm or tiny village with names she did not recognise – Polton Hambly… Ottington… Cambroke…

She didn't even know if there would be any people there. Ice needed to zoom out to see that she was twelve and a half miles west of Depton – a matter of mere minutes in a car, but a long trudge if you were already exhausted and your feet were soaked inside your trainers. Still, it was a comfort to see the name and to finally have some idea of where in the world she was. She could see, too, that the country lane was a little over three miles from a larger 'B' road, which, although it did not lead straight back to Depton itself, was at least part of the network and a sign of civilisation. Somewhere along it she should find houses or a petrol station or a shop open late and the hope of being able to contact her parents.

It can't have been more than twenty minutes after Ice had mustered her will and set off, that the moon descended completely and she was forced to use her phone as a torch. It afforded her a few hundred yards of light before it died and everything became a lot darker.

Chapter 27 ~ Samhain

For the first time since the car had crashed, Ice allowed herself the shedding of a few tears of exasperation. Crying was a self-indulgence she mainly tried to avoid. It usually meant she was tired or ill. Now, she felt both. Although it was not pitch black – there was still light in the sky from the distant fires – it was insufficient to see clearly and she found herself walking hesitantly, stumbling over the uneven ground. The road surface was more predictable but she could not bring herself to take the middle. It might have been deserted, but that made it more likely that a random driver would be speeding and not see her. So she made painfully slow progress along the right hand side, slipping where the scruffy edge of the tarmac met the verge in a series of ruts and bumps.

It was the wrong choice. Though she made her best effort to place her feet securely with each step, her legs were heavy with weariness and her reactions too slow. She could not see where water and heat had combined to erode a treacherous gulley in her path, only aware of the sudden loss of balance and the flare of pain as her ankle crumpled beneath her and she fell.

For a stunned half minute, Ice lay still on the plant tufts and pebbles by the side of the road. The searing pain took her breath away and she was furious at her own clumsiness. Broken or sprained – it made no difference. She had gone as far as she would go. She did not attempt to stand, nor to examine the injury. She did not move to a more comfortable location or further away from the road. Ice lay motionless on her side where she had fallen, and closed her eyes. She would try to go no further until dawn.

"You are such an idiot!" she berated herself in an angry whisper. Her ankle throbbed like a recrimination, proving her point, and she had a banging headache. She had not eaten all day and this morning felt like a lifetime away.

"A bit hasty sometimes, perhaps," came a quiet voice. "But you're never an idiot. It's just the way you are – the way you've always been, since I've known you, anyway. We wouldn't want you to be any different. Trying to save the little guys. It's what we love about you. You're a lot like my mum in that way!"

The air was warm, but Ice began to shiver uncontrollably.

"I miss you," she whispered.

"I know. I'm so sorry."

She felt the sensation of a gentle touch, like a hand stroking her hair away from her face. Perhaps it was just the breeze. Her shaking subsided momentarily.

"Always a big conspiracy for you to uncover!" he went on, laughing quietly. "Or sometimes it might not be. Sometimes it's the smallest of things... like when the aliens are defeated in 'War of the Worlds'. Some normal germs. Just an accidental cut. A cheeky little bacterium lurking, resistant to antibiotics. A missed sepsis. Nature does its stuff, reminding us that we're not special. We're just another blob of organic matter carrying around some DNA!"

"Some blobs are nicer than others," Ice replied. She was no longer filled with anger but grief flared like a sharp pain in her chest.

"Don't worry. You're going to be OK... you know... kept going by *curiosity*," he said. "It's almost certainly the reason you get to see things the rest of us don't. I remember the birds you showed me when were in school. You saw they were something special because you were looking. I was like everyone else – only seeing what I expected to see."

She remembered their conversation. Curiosity? Is that what it was? Is that what had kept her going? Every moment had brought something new. Possibilities she had not predicted. Encounters that had driven her on – saved her life. Was that so different from hope? It was, actually, she decided. Hope was a bland, vague, passive emotion. It didn't seek answers. It didn't try to improve things. This was a low point for humans, but could things get better? For her and for life on this planet, both seemingly so tiny and insignificant in the vastness of it all? It wouldn't by simply hoping, would it? But it could still be turned around. The universe was full of what we didn't know.

"It's always possible." It was like a reply to her unspoken questions. "Strange things do happen. Happy Halloween, Ice…" The words faded like the sigh of wind through the branches. A voice brought to life in this isolated place. It sounded like a goodbye.

****

The headlights were intense after the darkness, shattering Ice's reverie and forcing her to open and then immediately cover her eyes with her arm. As understanding distilled out of her confusion, she realised that a car had stopped in front of her on the road.

Raising her hand to her brow and squinting, Ice peered in the direction of the vehicle. It was large and vaguely familiar. Silhouetted in the beam of the headlights was a figure she recognised. Without needing to see more clearly and before the person spoke, Ice knew it was the farmer they had met in Bale. She groaned audibly. Could it not have been anyone else?

"Hey!" the farmer shouted, "Is someone there?"

What did she think? Ice wondered. That she was a bunch of old clothes someone had thrown by the side of the road. Ice didn't blame her. It was how she felt.

"Yes," It came out as a rather feeble squeak. It had been a while since she had spoken out loud. She drew a deep breath and tried again, more forcefully."

"Yes… I'm here… er. I'm lost… I mean, I got lost in the fire… and I've done something to my ankle. I was trying to get to the main road but I can't really walk. Would you be able to give me a lift?"

The sound of Ice's words had a catalysing effect. Perhaps the farmer hadn't really expected the bundle of clothes to speak because she made an exclamation and then quickly ran towards her. Ice had no power to resist being lifted off the ground and practically carried to the car. The woman was as strong as she looked.

The farmer had helped Ice up into the passenger seat, forcing the collie to move over and make room, before saying, "Your clothes are all damp! Have you been in the river? What happened? What are you doing all the way out here?"

Ice nodded her response and then, as expected, the farmer looked at her more closely in the inside light of the SUV.

"I've seen you, haven't I? You were the one hanging around my farm. What's going on? You were with someone. A boy. Why are you still out?"

"Yes," Ice replied, looking down. The collie was sniffing her clothes with great interest. Was it just the river he was picking up or could he smell the trace of the great horse that had carried Ice away from the fire?

"Yes. That was me. I mean, I was there but then we… I left. Um… I got lost and had to go in the river. That's why I'm wet." She paused, wondering how to explain further. "Are the sheep OK?" she asked quietly.

The farmer did not answer immediately. She went round the vehicle and climbed in on the driver's side.

"We were lucky," she said. "But it was close. We were just lucky. If the wind had not changed and turned the fire back on itself, I probably would have been too late. Could you close your door, please? I'm in a hurry – as you know – I need to get back to the farm. To the ponies and the other animals. I'm sorry, I can't do anything about you immediately – you'll just have to come with. Then is there someone we can contact to fetch you?"

Ice shook her head.

"No. I mean yes, my parents... but my phone is dead. I'm sorry – I mean the farm – it's gone. The fire reached it. We saw it go up. I'm so sorry. There won't be much left of Bale, anywhere there."

Chapter 28 ~ Project

ce's words seemed to suck all the energy out of her
companion. At first she did not respond, as though she
needed time to comprehend the reality of what Ice had just
revealed. Then, to Ice's dismay, the farmer's eyes welled up
with tears. She did not move but continued to stare in Ice's
direction as if she was not seeing her, but the horror in her
mind's eye.

She appeared to gradually gather her wits and then, needing
to articulate her thoughts, she said slowly, "The animals… My
ponies… Oh no. Poor creatures! I must go and see if there
was any chance they were spared!" This had the effect of
galvanising her back into action and she made to switch on the
motor and turn off the inside light but Ice stopped her.

"Wait! I mean, yes. You should return when you can and
see, but the animals are no longer there. We… uh… we…" Ice
hunted for the right words – did they 'steal' them or 'rescue'
them? "Well when we saw the fires, we let the ponies go. They
ran. I'm sure they knew which way to go to be safe. I'm sorry
– we didn't know what else to do. Their field was going to
burn."

"You let them go!" was the reply. Ice returned her gaze.
Was she angry or relieved? The woman sighed loudly.
"Whatever gave you the right to do that?"

Angry, then, Ice thought.

"I suppose I should thank you! Now I only have to go find
my animals that could be absolutely anywhere. Better than a
load of charred corpses, I suppose. Did you let *all* of them
go?"

"The wild ones in the cages?" Ice replied. She was so tired. Her head was throbbing because of the low blood sugar and the effects of smoke. The pain competed with that coming from her ankle and she felt nauseous. It was with some effort that she continued. "No, we didn't. Well not there… actually… I know where they might be. They might be safe. And free. Why were you keeping them in cages, anyway? They shouldn't be here, it's not really fair, is it?" She thought of Joe. Had he made it? If only she could call him or her parents. But her phone was dead. She didn't know anyone's number by heart or she could ask the farmer if she could borrow her phone. The woman was talking to her again.

"What do you mean? Where? How do you know…? Did you… have you done something with them? How is that possible? Those are valuable specimens! They need to be protected!"

It was too many questions through the brain fog. Another thought was congealing. It would help answer the questions and more.

"I need to phone," she said, weakly. "Do you have…?" she held up her dead mobile, pointing to the USB socket at the base. It was easier than getting out the words. The collie had given up sniffing and had curled up, laying his head on her lap. She envied him.

The farmer looked at Ice's device, seeming to collect her thoughts and remember her compassion; here was a lost, hurt kid that needed help more than an interrogation. She nodded.

"Yes, of course. I think so. Sorry, you must be exhausted and…". She leant across Ice and reached into a glove compartment. She rummaged around and pulled out something wrapped in plastic and a black cord.

"Are you hungry?" she handed Ice the objects. "I'm Mrs Williamson. Chris. And you?" She turned the engine back on. "See if that fits. I'll leave the engine on to charge it. Let's find a better place to stop."

Ice took the gifts gratefully. She had stuffed the cake bar in her mouth before seeing, to her great relief, that the USB charger was the right size for her phone and plugging it into the socket on the dashboard. Mrs Williamson drove the vehicle a little way up the road and pulled into a small lay-by.

"Ice… Cooper," Ice said, swallowing cake and watching the screen light up before giving her full name. "Isis." At this point, she was no longer trying to hide her identity. They both needed to be straight with each other.

A flurry of pings came from her phone as multiple messages and missed calls registered. It was almost a shock to see that there was a signal at last. Ice wasn't sure who to start with. She had to find out what had happened with the animals and she also had to speak to her parents. The thought filled her with hope and with dread. She had been so reckless.

***

It was taking a while from Ice's apprehensive phone call till her parents could get to them in their car, loaded with items and people, and with the trailer attached. She had spoken to her father. He had not said much after the initial outburst of shock, relief, and the demand to know where the hell she was.

Frantic phone calls had, of course, not reached her and they had been unable to do anything but wait in the hope that she would eventually turn up, delivered by some unnamed person. According to Joe's testimony, she had been OK when he had spoken to her, hours ago, driving away from the fire, but she had been in the car of a complete stranger. The police had already been informed.

She knew she should have been with them on their way north by now. It was her fault that their plans had been disrupted and they were having to make this detour. It was hard to wait for them. The cake bar had restored her only a little and now she just wanted to lie down somewhere and push away her feelings of guilt. She could not do that though. She had to explain to the farmer what they had done and to show her the location of Baycote where Joe, somehow, according to his message, had managed to be successful.

Mrs Williamson was still talking, half to herself.

"I just don't know where they all came from. I know it's been dry, but really...! They just seemed to spring up all over... And my farm. What's left? And the preservation project. Already Asa was on the loose. Now how will I find all the others. If they've even survived..."

Ice was looking at the photograph of the panther.

"Is this Asa? He's OK. At least he was when I last saw him. He got out of the river where I did." She did not mention the horse.

"That's him!" Mrs Williamson exclaimed. "You've seen him! I've tried recapture without telling the authorities. He doesn't deserve to be shot because of my carelessness. Such a clever animal. Like his grandmother. She got out once. Created a lot of legends before we got her back. Asa outwitted me and continues to do so. This was my husband's project but he died last year and I'm afraid I've barely managed since – as you saw. The sheep and the farm. It's too much for one person."

"Project?" Ice asked.

"The GSPP – Global Species Preservation Project" the farmer explained. "Graham was always concerned about wildlife. He hated the idea of whole species being wiped out. This was his way of trying to help. We are like 'foster parents'. There are lots of us – farmers and zoos around the world to try to preserve endangered species. We help by keeping small numbers of animals in low-key settings, the idea being that by distributing them, they are increasing the chance of some surviving if any single location fails, and they're semi secret – away from the traffickers. Meanwhile there was work to restore habitats so that they could return them to the wild. It was a last ditch attempt to prevent extinction. Have you ever heard of Père David's Deer?"

Ice shook her head. She didn't think so. She was interested to hear that there were people still working on restoring habitats. Her recent experiences had given her the impression that destruction was unchecked.

"They lived in China and were wiped out by foreign soldiers in the 19th Century. But there were some that were in captivity in Europe. Eventually, in the 1980s they were able to be reintroduced to China. They survive successfully in nature reserves there."

Ice supposed it made sense. Not putting all your 'eggs' in one basket. It seemed incredibly careless to her, though. How did they vet their 'foster parents'? Not only had Mrs Williamson let Asa escape, but she had risked all the animals by leaving them unattended when there were fires threatening. She was clearly overwhelmed with the task.

"I'm not sure about the birds," Ice said, "but you… they… whoever… might be able to find the animals again if they need to. I think they're here."

Ice held the phone so that the farmer could see the map on the screen. She double tapped to zoom in on Baycote.

"My friend… we were going to take them somewhere away from the fires to be safe. You're lucky we were there or they'd have died in their cages."

There was bitterness in her voice. She felt too tired for sympathy and she felt no guilt about taking the animals. It was true that she and Joe had saved those creatures from a horrible death, trapped where they had no cause to be.

Ice looked at the other recent pictures on her phone and stopped at the photograph of the poor Elena in the bunker at Bale. Behind her were the lit screens of the computers. Ice vaguely remembered Elena's distressed phone conversation with an unknown respondent. She spread the image larger with her thumb and finger and peered at the screen. In the bottom left corner was a logo – one that she knew very well – a bright blue 'K' with rounded silver edges – the company symbol for Konnara Industries. The company where her father had worked as a shale gas engineer. The company that had hidden reports on earthquakes – the ones her mother had found. The company her mother was giving evidence against. Ice turned to Mrs Williamson.

"What do you think is meant by 'burn zones'?" she asked.

There was a voice calling her name. A familiar voice. Ice sat up, feeling guilt and embarrassment, but mostly the wonderful sense of safety, once she was wrapped in her mother's arms. Her father was in conversation with Mrs Williamson. She could hear snatches of sentences – a mixture of polite gratitude and query. The woman was somewhat nonplussed. She did not have all the details of Ice's adventure that Mr Cooper seemed to expect from her. There was a brief exchange of contact information. He turned back to Ice.

What the actual hell…?" he started. "Ice, what were you thinking? You could have been killed. We had no idea what had happened or where you were. Can you imagine what we've been going through? Are you hurt? Come on, let's get you to the car!"

Her mother was silent, already getting her to her feet and pulling Ice's arm around her shoulder so that she could help her limp to the waiting vehicle. Mrs Cooper's face was illuminated in the beam of the lights but Ice could not read her expression. She had every right to be very angry with her, she knew. Any apology would be insufficient. Her mother caught her glance and shook her head.

"Later," she said, briefly. "There'll be plenty of time for that when we're away from here."

It was absolute bliss to get to the car. Once out of the dazzling beam, Ice saw that it was loaded to the hilt. There was just enough room for Buddy, squeezed in next to linen in the back and wriggling frantically, 'punching' the back window at Ice's approach. Joe opened the rear left door and stepped out so that Ice could slide in next to her brother who was staring at her with an expression of disbelief mixed with admiration. He grinned and waved his phone in triumph, pointing at the map location. Then he tipped his head forward as though peering over a pair of imaginary glasses and gave her a 'stern' look of mock admonishment for being in trouble. It was brilliant to see him and she gratefully accepted his proffered water bottle and half-eaten bread and cheese.

Joe squeezed in next to Ice so that she was sandwiched in the middle. She was sore and still damp, but she did not care. She leaned her head back against the seat.

Mr Cooper pulled the car round in a difficult U-turn with the trailer on the small lane, and headed for the main road. As he reached the junction, there was a sound like a distant clap of thunder and then a delay before the car windows rattled with the shock-wave of one huge explosion shortly followed by another. Joe swore loudly, forgetting to moderate his language in front of the adults, and gripped Ice's hand. Her dad pulled the car to a stop. It was miles away in Bale, but they could all see the bright yellow flames rolling high up into the night sky. Joe looked at Ice, eyes wide.

"Is that where we…?" he began. Ice interrupted him with a nod. They were all staring at her with expressions of mixed horror and interrogation.

"It's a long story," she said. Maybe later she would have to give a full explanation but right now she could not face it. "But we should just go," she said, grateful that there were no more questions and that her father was already putting the car into gear and moving off. It made it rather awkward for Ice's mother to lean over from the front seat and get a look at the damage to Ice's ankle. Mrs Cooper had pulled out a bandage and one of her own dressing gowns from the bag in the footwell, so that Ice was strapped up and, with some discreet wriggling, out of her damp clothes by the time they got to the main road.

***

The boy on her left was talking. Words had been tumbling out in a way that Ice had not experienced from him before. They were well on to the motorway when he finally finished telling her how he had reached Baycote Reservoir in his mum's boyfriend's van. How he had to use the bolt-cutters on the lock of the gate which closed off the slim roadway to the central island. How he had twice nearly driven them all off into the water but that he had made it and opened the cages. How the animals were at first anxious and wary and he had thought he would have to drag the cages on to the ground and leave them with their doors open so that they could vacate in their own time, but that almost simultaneously they had sensed freedom and escaped their prisons.

"It was pretty cool, Ice," he continued his quiet monologue. "It was like they suddenly knew what to do." He laughed. "I wish you could have seen them scampering off into the undergrowth as though they didn't believe their luck! You would have loved the parrots in the trees. It was so weird – all bright blue and exotic. Maybe they'll breed and we'll have macaws in England!"

Ice let him rattle on. She knew you weren't supposed to release non-native species into the countryside. If they survived and bred and dispersed, they could disrupt the whole ecosystem. But that ship felt like it had already sailed. The climate had seen to that. The farmer knew they were there, anyway. She almost wished she didn't – wild animals should not live in cages – but maybe they had a small chance of surviving and being put back in their natural environment. She knew Mrs Williamson had been telling the truth. She just wasn't sure how hopeful that was.

Joe was holding her hand again. She had the other one clasped tightly by her little brother, even though he had managed to curl himself up with his head on the door hand-rest and looked to be asleep. It was awkwardly comforting and Ice did not wish to upset the two boys either side of her, so she let her hands remain, unable to brush away the tears that now fell freely for that other boy. The one that she had lost.

A light drizzle fell – 'soft rain' the Scots called it – her favourite type of weather. She had awoken early and now stood in the kitchen gazing absent-mindedly out of the cottage window while she waited for the kettle to boil on the ancient-looking stove. She made no noise, so as not to disturb Buddy, still curled up on his bed, paws twitching as he played chase in his dreams. The smell of wood-smoke could still recall that night, although now it had become increasingly associated with the comfort of their new home. Nevertheless, she was inclined to keep the window open, or to stand in the doorway so that she could breathe the sweet, clean air, and after a time, her lungs had felt nearly normal again.

It was exactly a year since she had been rescued from the forest fires. A year in which nothing had been the same as before, but everything had been grounded in a much deeper sense of reality by comparison.

Joe had stayed. Her parents had simply accepted him into the fold. She often found him working quietly alongside her father, helping to dig the ground or construct make-shift greenhouses for the plants. He appeared to like the practical things. Ice was aware of the common experiences that Joe and her father shared, but neither of them talked about those and she kept her knowledge to herself.

Mia had been in contact. Ice would never stop being grateful for digital technology and the infrastructure that remained – it had literally been a life-saver and now it allowed her to keep in touch with her friend. The rest of Ice's lifestyle would not have looked out of place in a previous century, though. They grew their own food and kept their own chickens for eggs. Much of the repairs to the cottage had been made with local materials and the same tools people had used for a hundred years – longer for those that did not need electricity. In contrast, Mia's parents were working on the technology of the future. From her texts and video calls, Ice understood them to be developing sustainable systems to harness renewable energy and tackle the changes in the environment wrought by the climate. She seemed back to her upbeat self. Ice missed her company.

Oscar was grateful to have a working phone, too. Sometimes he still lost himself in a simulated world, but increasingly, she noticed he chose other activities. When he wasn't mucking in with the work, he could sometimes be found running across the dunes with Buddy, who was delighted – all that freedom and all those new smells. Oscar had started to capture photographs of birds, using the pictures to make finely-detailed pencil drawings back at the cottage.

She had been right about the symbol she had seen and without her photographs, all the evidence of Konnara Industries would most likely have been destroyed by the fire. The fires that they themselves had set. It was the kind of behaviour that Ice and others had come to expect of large companies fighting to maintain their grip and their business as fossil fuels became ever more problematic. Even so, it was outrageous. There was the ongoing court case in which her mother was giving evidence, but still they had continued to plan further drilling operations in the area, moving equipment to nearby locations and surreptitiously bringing chemicals in unmarked lorries to storage facilities. Like Bale.

The supposed suspension of activities hadn't stopped the company from looking for loopholes in the law. They might halted drilling for the moment, but they were busy prospecting. Land that was designated greenbelt was supposedly protected and they were not permitted to carry out any fracking near residential areas, but a recent change in the law allowed for so-called 'redevelopment' of places that had been devastated by fires.

Ice had washed her hands of it, having passed on all her evidence to people better equipped to use it. Maybe this time Konnara might not sidestep the law quite so easily. The fires they had set could be linked to them through the 'burn zones' map – areas marked out and dated *before* there had actually been any fires. She wasn't sure how much was left at the depot at Bale because the chemicals being stored there had gone up in the explosion. Thirty-seven people, including Elena Nicolescu, had lost their lives. It had been an expensive operation for the emergency services, already stretched to breaking point, and the clear up of Bale and the surrounding area was likely to take some time. The whole of Depton had been evacuated and many people had lost their homes to the flames. Some were claiming that it had been deliberate. That they had meant to move people out to get round the issue of fracking in a residential area. It may have been a bit far-fetched, but the fires had not stayed in their 'burn zones'. If nothing else, there would be claims against the company for compensation. Not that they could ever compensate for the environmental destruction. All those trees. All that wildlife. By rights, the directors should face imprisonment at the very least. Ice hoped that there was still sufficient, uncorrupted legal power to see it through, but she was not sure.

She was lost in these thoughts as Oscar quietly joined her and followed her gaze across the vegetable plots and through the finely-sifting rain. The day had yet to break, though light was just beginning to show on the horizon below the clouds. It made the view from the window resemble a pastel drawing with features smudged in darker shades of blue and grey.

Oscar screwed up his eyes and leaned forward at the open window.

"Is there somebody there?" he asked, peering out.

Ice smiled and nodded, keeping her gaze fixed on the figure by the stone wall at the end of their 'garden'. It was too dark to see detail and it could have been a trick of the twilight, but Ice did not think so. She raised her hand in a gesture of recognition, and saw a waved response, just as the sun rose, breaking through the clouds. For a moment it seemed to pick out a mop of blond hair before the garden was filled with the dawn light.

"Oh!" Oscar said, rubbing his eyes to refocus. "Oh well, he's gone now, but I could have sworn there was someone standing there. Maybe it was just a ghost!" He laughed as though dismissing it as a trick of the imagination after all. Ice nodded.

"Yes," she said, softly to herself. "Maybe."

ACKNOWLEDGEMENT

Many thanks to my daughter, Ayla who is always my first beta reader and to Ash, for plot feedback. Thanks also to those who were eager to read this next instalment of the Ice Cooper series and kept nagging me to finish. I would also like to express appreciation to my editors for their useful work and encouragement.

ABOUT THE AUTHOR

J A Bowler

J A Bowler was born in Zimbabwe but now lives in Warwickshire and often draws on the local environment in story settings. Having taught primary aged children for the best part of three decades, the author is now a freelance writer and artist who also sometimes plays in bands on saxophones and bass guitar.

Please connect (and sign up to my mailing list) on:

Author site: jabowler.co.uk

Social media:

Twitter: twitter.com/JBowler_author
Instagram: www.instagram.com/jabowlerauthor/
Facebook: www.facebook.com/JABowler

Email: julietbowler@outlook.com

Reviews are the lifeblood of authors, and you have my deep gratitude if you leave one for Ice Cooper and the Beast of Bale or any of my books.

Also by J A Bowler

Ice Cooper and the Depton Shadelings

Rainswept Depton is a town with dark secrets. New to the area, young teen, Ice Cooper is alarmed to see the strange creatures from her dreams. When the earthquakes start and people go missing, she is forced out of her comfort zone. She knows when people are lying, so what is her own father hiding? And where is her mother? Ice may need help from her new friends and an unlikely source if she is to survive and discover the truth.

This YA supernatural eco-thriller is the first in the Ice Cooper series.

The Improbable Adventures of Dexter Duckworth.

When Dexter the duckling falls into the Duckworth's pond, he finds a comfortable, friendly home. But one day, he and his boy, James get taken to Goblin Earth. They'll have to save each other and solve the problem of the goblin changeling back home. Help comes from an unexpected source, though it'll be a challenging and dangerous adventure. Dexter would rather watch old films on telly, but he and James both know you don't abandon your friends.

A magical adventure book for children aged 6-11 years.

Springtail